MYSTIC MOONHAVEN MYSTERIES

VOLUME 1

# DAISY LANDISH

Editing by Jessica McKenna
Cover by Daisy Landish

BEACHES AND TRAILS
PUBLISHING

# ALSO BY DAISY LANDISH

**Clean Regency Romance**

The Lady Series - The Allington Collection

The Lady Series - The Gillingham Collection

The Lady Series - The Blackmore Collection

The Lady Series - The Norrington Collection

**Clean Contemporary Romance**

Love on Spruce Island

Second Chance

Cherry Tree Island

The Wedding Trio

Extra Credit

Counting on the Cowboy

Focusing on the Cowboy

Mistletoe Magic

Grounded at Christmas

**Cozy Mysteries**

Jane and Kennedy Daniels Mysteries

Pine Grove Mysteries

Annie Archer Paranormal Mysteries

Wilma Wade Holiday Mysteries

Mike and Maddie Mysteries

Mystic Moonhaven Mysteries

Sweater Weather: Cozy Mysteries for Fall

Summer Vibes: Cozy Mysteries for Summer

Let it Snow: Cozy Mysteries for Winter

# ABOUT THE AUTHOR

Daisy Landish is a romance and cozy mystery author living in the UK, whose clean and sweet stories have tugged at readers' heartstrings across the pond and beyond. When she's not writing, Daisy spends her time reading, hiking at dawn, and riding into the sunset on her horse, Rosebud.

Join Daisy's Newsletter for updates and giveaways!
www.daisylandishromance.com

facebook.com/daisylandishromance

x.com/daisy_landish

instagram.com/beachesandtrailspublishing

amazon.com/author/daisylandish

bookbub.com/authors/daisy-landish

goodreads.com/Daisy_Landish

# 1

## FROSTY BEGINNINGS

As I fastened my nametag to my shirt, I couldn't help but reminisce. It had been a year since I uprooted my life to settle in Moonhaven, a decision driven more by instinct than reason. My new identity as Harper Nightshade, owner of the town's only occult bookstore, 'Nightshade's Nook,' felt as surreal as the mystical tomes lining its shelves.

The crisp winter air seeped through the cracks as I flicked on the radio, letting cheerful tunes displace the morning silence. Mondays were my sanctuary from the usual hustle—no regular hours, just me and my beloved store. Today, I planned to transform this sanctuary for the Winter Festival. Climbing the ladder, I reached for the 'Happy New Year' banner, but a sudden chill crept down my spine, an all-too-familiar frosty touch that spoke of unseen presences.

Heart pounding, I scanned the room, every shadow and corner. My shop, a cozy haven of ancient books and arcane artifacts, seemed unchanged, yet the air felt charged as if a whisper from the other world lingered just beyond my perception. I eyed the evergreen garlands and the small tree on the cashier's counter, remnants of a Christmas celebrated with my own blend of tradition and witchcraft.

The bell above the door jangled, snapping me back to reality. I spun around, losing my footing on the ladder. A scream escaped my lips as I braced for the fall.

Strong arms caught me, steadying me before I could hit the ground. I found myself looking into the concerned eyes of Detective Liam Ashford. His presence, unexpected yet oddly reassuring, sent a wave of heat to my cheeks.

"Are you alright, Harper?" His voice was laced with genuine concern.

"Yes, thank you, Detective." I managed to steady my voice, though my heart still raced—whether from the fall or his proximity, I couldn't tell. He removed his knitted hat, revealing the perfectly tousled hair that somehow added to his magazine-worthy appearance. "I noticed the lights on. Thought I'd check in." I nodded, feeling a mix of gratitude and embarrassment. "I'm redecorating for the festival. Should've locked the door, though."

"Speaking of which, be extra careful these mornings," he said, his tone shifting to professional concern. "We've had reports of wolves in town. And if you notice any strange people lurking around, let me know."

Wolves? In Moonhaven? The news sent another shiver through me, though this time, it wasn't from any spectral chill. "I haven't seen anything amiss. But something does feel off."

Liam raised an eyebrow, his usual skepticism surfacing. "You mean beyond wildlife concerns?"

"It's hard to explain. It's like a... frost in the air," I said, careful not to mention the spectral presence I had sensed. "A feeling that something is about to happen."

His smile was a blend of amusement and disbelief. "Mystical energy, Harper?"

"Maybe," I replied a little defensively. "There's more to this world than what we see. Sometimes, you have to trust your instincts."

He pondered my words for a moment, then nodded. "Just stay safe. And call if anything unusual comes up." As he headed for the door, the sense of an unseen presence faded, leaving me alone with my thoughts and a store in need of decoration. But Liam's visit had stirred something within me—a realization that my connection to Moonhaven ran deeper than mere chance. I resumed my task, my mind buzzing with questions and the frosty touch of the unknown still lingering at the edge of my awareness.

There was a palpable reason Moonhaven reserved its Winter Festival for the cruelest months of January. The relentless cold had a way of seeping into the soul, inspiring a kind of introspection that bordered on the mystical, even for those who didn't dabble in the occult.

I was pulled by these macabre thoughts by the door again. It swung open to reveal Abigail Thorne, her grey hair a silver crown beneath a hand-knitted hat. Her smile was a beacon in the frosty air, warming the room instantly.

"Ah, Detective! Always a pleasure," she greeted, wrapping Liam in a hug that spoke of a lifelong familiarity.

Out of everyone in town, Abigail was pretty much the only person who could get away with something like that. It helped that she owned the Bed and Breakfast that most newcomers end up staying at while they find a permanent place to live. I was still there, renting out a room at a much-reduced price. Unfortunately, the housing market in Moonhaven left much to be desired.

Liam had known her his whole life. He gave her an indulgent smile.

"It's good to see you, too," he told her. "I have to be on my way, though. I'll be by the B&B later to fix that leaking sink."

"You're a gem, Liam," she replied, her eyes twinkling with a mirth that seemed to know too much.

Liam left, and I shut the door after him, locking it.

"Things still seem to be frosty between you, too," Abigail noted.

I shrugged. "We just don't get along. It's one of those things."

"I always thought you two would get along famously."

Oh, she was fishing for information. I hesitated; the truth of everything seemed to be rather infantile whenever I tried to explain it out loud. I'd only told my best friend from Moonhaven, Ella. Abigail had tried to wheedle the information from me before, but I'd been closed-lipped.

I sighed. No point in holding onto the secret forever. "The day I had my grand opening, he called my store 'hooky' and said that I was peddling nonsense. I got mad at him and told him he was born under a bad sign, and he laughed. I don't even know why I said that."

Sure, he had no way of knowing I was a witch, but he insulted my livelihood. Nobody in town knew I was a witch. It was the one thing I had always been extra careful to keep a secret.

"He said that to your face?" Abigail asked, her eyes widening.

I blushed. "He didn't know I was the owner. And he apologized. But he's so practical. I like to act on my gut. So, we just can't get along."

I busied myself, taking down some decorations at eye level to avoid Abigail's gaze. She looked amused, which wasn't exactly the best sign. What was she thinking? I couldn't imagine anything good. She had a reputation in town for being a little eccentric.

"It doesn't matter, anyway," I blurted. "He was just here to ask if I'd seen anything weird. There are apparently wolves around. Or at least, people think they're seeing wolves."

I shrugged.

Abigail nodded once. "Just remember, frost is just the beginning, my dear."

A shiver ran down my spine. I turned toward Abigail fully, squinting. "What do you mean by that?"

Abigail chuckled and shuffled toward the door. "I think I'll head over to the coffee shop. A nice hot coffee will do just the trick to warm up these aching bones. I'll be out late tonight, dear. I'll have a casserole in the fridge that you can heat."

"Thanks," I said, frowning.

She gave me an enigmatic smile before she unlocked the door and strode toward the coffee shop across the street.

What was that about? Frost is just the beginning... Was it about the weird energy that is permeating Moonhaven or between Liam and me? Which, honestly, that had a lot of weird energy, too. I thought it must be because my magic was bouncing off and being repelled by his skepticism.

I locked the door behind Abigail. Eccentric, yes, but she was a kindred spirit. She was a wonderful person and had made me feel so welcome in the town when I first moved here. Which I desperately needed... I'd moved shortly after the deaths of my parents, using my inheritance to open up this store.

Even now, as much as I loved the town and my store, I would give anything to have my parents back.

The lights went out.

I jumped as a chill washed down my back again. The pale morning light filtered through the blinds, barely enough to light the interior of my store. I held my hand palm out and whispered an incantation. A flame jumped to life, warming my face.

Normal spirits can't interact with the world like turning off lights... was this a poltergeist?

"Alright, whatever you are," I called out. "I'm not interested in playing games. Turn the lights back on, or I'll have to get nasty."

My threat reverberated in the empty store. I headed for the front desk, observing anything that might fall on my head. Once I was there, I held the flame over the drawer, looking for the master switch for the lights.

Something caught my eye on the little Christmas tree. A man's face reflected in one globe. I gasped and leaned closer—

A wind burst through the shop, knocking books off the shelf. My flame blew out at once.

# A DISAPPEARANCE IN THE SNOW

The next day, instead of going straight to the bookstore, I headed to *Ella's Wheel*, the best coffee shop in Moonhaven. I had to say it was the best, because my best friend, Ella, was the owner of the place. It was the best, though, even if I might be biased.

Ella must have seen the cloud hanging over my head as I took my normal seat, frowning. She slid a sugar cookie to me.

"I'll be back soon," she promised me. "I have a couple of other orders to fill first."

I nodded at her. "Take your time. I'm in no hurry."

I spun the cookie on the plate. Normally, I'd jump at the opportunity to eat sugar for breakfast, but today, I was too involved in the events that happened yesterday. Who was the spirit I'd seen in my bookstore, and why was he here?

The building was new, so it couldn't be a long-dead person emerging. Maybe he was drawn to the bookstore by the energy of my magic? That didn't explain the cold and how the lights went out, though. Spirits usually can't do that sort of thing.

There was something weird happening, and I didn't like it.

Ella returned to me and handed me a large cup of coffee prepared just the way I liked it.

"Did you know him?" she asked me with a sympathetic look.

I frowned at her. "Who?"

"David Blackwood. He's been reported as missing."

"What? When?"

I'd never met him personally, but it seemed like everyone around town knew him. He ran the museum and archives. I'd seen quite a few newspaper articles about various books he published on the history of Moonhaven and the people who lived here.

"This morning. Apparently, his roommate hadn't seen him for a few days and got worried when he didn't answer his phone," Ella told me, lowering her voice slightly. "Detective Liam found his car at the museum. It was still covered in that snow we got a few days ago."

I shivered as I processed this information. How horrible would it be to be missing for days and have nobody realize it?

"If his car was at the museum, where is he?" I asked.

Ella shook her head. "Nobody knows. That's why he's missing. There's no way to know if someone kidnapped him or if he got lost in the forest."

"Or maybe the books finally ate him," a voice on my other side said.

I turned to see Percival Whitman sitting there, looking amused. The Whitmans were the closest thing Moonhaven had to royalty. They were one of the founding families of the town and still owned over half of the property here. Percival had never worked a day in his life; all his income came from renting out the land to farmers and shop owners.

I was fortunate enough to own the store. Otherwise, I'd be paying the slimeball through the nose to stay in business.

"It's a wonder we even noticed he was missing," Percival drawled. "That nerd would stay in the museum for weeks at a time. Was never late for rent, though, so who am I to complain?"

Ella sighed. "Is that a subtle reminder that my rent is coming up due, Percy?"

"Not at all." Percival gave her a toothy grin. "I don't care if you're late, Ella. Where else am I going to find such delicious coffee than what you brew?"

I rolled my eyes at the obvious flirting. Ella wasn't interested in

Percival, but that didn't stop him. Luckily, he seemed to be content to keep it at flirting, but I already told Ella that we could put an addition on my bookstore for a new coffee shop if she wanted to.

"We're all hoping that Detective Liam will find David soon," Ella said, refilling Percival's mug.

"Of course, of course," Percival said.

He waved a hand and sauntered away.

Ella released a heavy breath and focused on me again. "Anyway. From what I've heard, David might have been in over his head in some financial crisis. Some people say that he faked his death to escape a debt he owes to the mob."

"That doesn't seem very likely." I sipped at my coffee, frowning. "Do you have a picture of him? I'm not sure I know what he looks like."

"Of course. Here." Ella whipped her phone from her apron pocket and started scrolling on it.

After a few minutes, she handed it to me. She had pulled up the museum website. Right at the bottom was a picture of David Blackwood. He had kind eyes and a solemn expression as he clasped a book to his chest.

I gasped.

It was the same man I'd seen in my bookshop yesterday. Dread filled me. Did that mean that David was dead? Had he sought me out to help find his body and bring him to peace?

"What's wrong?" Ella asked, peering around the counter at the frown. "Did one of my fanfic tabs open instead?"

I forced out a laugh at her joke and handed her the phone back. "Sorry. No, I just realized I know him. It's just so unnerving, you know? When this happens to someone you know."

It wasn't a great excuse, but it was the only one that I could think of. Nobody knew I was a witch. Ever since I was a kid, my parents drilled it into me that nobody could know. Even if these days witches were thought of in a generally more positive light than, say, the sixteen-hundreds, it was still dangerous to let anyone know.

My stomach curled around the little bit of coffee I'd put into it.

He wasn't just missing. He was dead. And he was coming to me for help. What could I do, though? I wasn't an investigator. Even if I found his body, how would I tell Liam about it? He'd probably think I was a suspect!

On the other hand, I had to do something. I hated the thought of David's spirit being lost in the cold like this.

"I wish I could get into the museum and look around," I said aloud. "Maybe I could help Liam somehow."

Percival spoke up again, proving he'd been eavesdropping on us still. "I have a key. It's my land and my building, after all. Here." He fished a keychain from his pocket, detached one, and handed it to me. "I'd like to see David back safe and sound, too."

"Thanks." I tucked the key into my pocket.

Ella shot me a 'be careful' warning look before she was called away. I wished I could bring her with me, but she was busy. I finished my coffee and headed out.

The museum was empty, as expected, when I arrived. I unlocked the front door and stepped in. A blast of icy air hit me, and I sucked in a hard breath. It was colder inside the museum than it was outside! I pulled my cap down over my ears and stepped in, looking around cautiously.

The sound of a car crunching the snow in the driveway made me spin. Liam's sleek cruiser pulled up and stopped. Even before he got out of the car, he frowned at me.

"What are you doing here?" he demanded when he joined me at the entrance.

"Percival Whitman gave me a key," I said, holding it up as proof. "I thought maybe I could help."

Liam pulled off his hat and ran his fingers through his hair. "This is the last thing I need—a bunch of hicks mucking up my investigation."

I stiffened. "Hicks?"

"Sorry. I didn't mean it like that." He actually looked abashed, which eased my indignation. "Only if Whitman goes around giving keys to whoever asks, that means my list of suspects is blown wide open."

I looked at the key in my hand. "He just gave it to me at the coffee shop. Ella has cameras if you need to check."

Liam shook his head. "You aren't a suspect, Harper. Just don't interfere in my investigation."

"I can help."

"You don't have the training."

I put my fists on my hips. "And maybe you rely too much on your training. There's such a thing as intuition, you know."

Liam's frown deepened. The tension simmered between us like a pot of water ready to boil. Finally, he waved his hand at the museum's interior.

"Alright, you can look around. Don't touch anything. If you see anything that looks out of place, take a picture and then find me. Got it?"

I nodded. "Yes, sir."

Liam rolled his eyes, but it looked like he was fighting a laugh.

He headed across the room to turn on the thermostat, and I held my hand out, palm-up. Watching to make sure Liam wouldn't catch on, I whispered a spell, calling on my searching wind. A breeze picked up around me, tugging at my hair. To anyone else, it would look like I was standing in a draft.

I followed the wind to behind David's desk. There, on the floor, was a single brass button.

"I found something," I called.

"Already?" Liam asked, sounding startled.

"There's a button on the floor here." I whipped out my phone and snapped a picture.

Liam came over, putting on latex gloves. He snapped a picture as well before he picked up the button. As he turned it this way and that, it caught the lights.

David's face flared on the brassy surface. His eyes were enormous, and his mouth moved as though he was shouting something.

An icy wind hit me in the square of my back, and I gasped.

Liam caught my elbow. "What's wrong?"

His eyes skimmed through the museum, searching for what set me off. I was so shocked at the protectiveness that he displayed that I forgot to answer at first. I only gaped at him as though that wasn't suspicious at all.

When he finally met my gaze again, he arched one of his brown eyebrows at me. "What's wrong?" he repeated.

"Nothing," I said, rolling my shoulders to lose the tension in them. "There was just a sudden shivery feeling. I guess the furnace must be pushing out the cold air."

Liam studied me like he wasn't sure if he believed me.

I cleared my throat, blushing. Even if I told him about what I just saw, he wouldn't believe me. Just knowing that tempted me to blurt out everything, but that wouldn't help. I needed to get back to town and see if I could contact David's spirit directly. It was clear he wasn't just hanging around my shop now.

Something bigger than a disappearance was happening here.

"I think you're right; I shouldn't be poking around here," I said, stepping backward toward the door. "I don't want to do anything that might jeopardize your case."

If I could contact David, though, I'd nudge Liam in the right direction. Right now, however, poking around the museum was a bad idea.

"On the other hand, you know now that Percival Whitman will hand out keys willy-nilly," I added. "I'm sorry for taking up your time."

Liam grabbed my hand before I could leave. He squeezed lightly, making goosebumps break out along my arm.

"Take care of yourself, Harper," he told me.

I smiled, touched by his concern. "I will. Promise."

···•··

I spent the rest of the day trying to contact David's spirit without success. This whole thing was super frustrating. David had come to me twice already, yet when I tried to contact him, nothing. It only proved that something weird was happening. But what? I still had no idea.

I plopped onto the couch next to Ella, sighing heavily. I was exhausted from my repeated attempts to contact David, so I was glad she was here and giving me an excuse to get some downtime.

"Are you okay?" she asked me, a crease furrowing her brow.

"Tired. I've been feeling off all day," I told her.

Ella nodded as she flicked through our saved movies. "Do you want to reschedule, then?"

"No. A couple of rom-coms is exactly what I need," I told her. "But remind me tomorrow I need to finish putting up those garlands that the town gave me for the winter festival. I'm looking forward to the parade. I think the fireworks are going to help take the frost out of the air."

Ella selected a movie we'd previously decided on. "Yeah, it's always a lot of fun. January is rough, and this year, it's rougher. Detective Liam found a button in the museum, but so far no news about who the killer is."

I shuddered. "Let's not talk about that."

"Sorry."

Abigail bustled into my room, carrying with her a tray of finger food. She set it down on the coffee table and took up her usual spot in the chair. "What are we talking about, dears?"

"The Winter Festival," I answered.

"Ah. Terrible that it's being overshadowed by this dreadful business." Abigail shook her head. "I still have faith that dear David might be found alive."

I had to look away.

"We're trying not to talk about that," Ella told Abigail. "Hey, did you know that the Winter Festival started because of a local folktale? That's why it happens in January in the middle of winter rather than at the start of winter."

Grateful for the distraction and always eager to learn more about it, I leaned forward. "Oh? What's the tale."

Abigail made a tutting noise. "Now, I'm not sure we should dredge up the old legends. Sometimes these things are made more powerful by talking about them."

I turned, wanting to ask what she meant, but before I could, Ella laughed.

"What powers? It's just a story. It all happened in sixteen-sixteen, ten years after Moonhaven was founded. It started with mysterious disappearances; people snatched out of their homes in the dead of night with no trace of them left behind," Ella said, lowering her voice.

Disappearances like David Blackwood.

"Then the bodies popped up. It was clear from the wounds that a ravaging pack of wolves was wandering the area, killing anyone in their path. The town grew frantic to protect themselves and set traps, but they were set off at night with no tracks around. Talk of an evil spirit in the area flourished."

"Oooh, I don't like this," I said anxiously. "Yesterday, Liam told me that people were seeing wolves around town."

Ella looked mildly interested. "Did he? When did you talk to him?"

"He came to her store," Abigail said. "I saw them when he left. They seemed to have a very close discussion."

"Oh?" Ella looked thrilled.

I shook my head. "Just finish the story."

Abigail sighed as she sipped her tea.

"Right." Ella cleared her throat. "Anyway. It all culminated in the disappearance of Penelope Whitman."

My eyes widened. "Whitman?"

"Yeah. She was the wife of whoever founded Moonhaven. I forget his name. Percival is a direct descendant of Penelope."

I processed that information. It seemed important, but how? I already knew that the Whitmans had founded Moonhaven. Maybe the museum held something that belonged to Penelope Whitman? It might be a connection.

"Anyway, after Penelope Whitman disappeared, all the strange things in town stopped. There were no more disappearances or deaths," Ella said, leaning back on the couch. "They found and trapped all the wolves in the area, too."

"Oh. That's a bit of an anti-climatic ending," I said.

Ella shrugged. "That's the story. She disappeared, and everything stopped. So, people ran around saying that she was a witch and caused it all. Especially after the witch hunts started in Salem."

I winced hard at that. I couldn't verify, since I didn't have the records of other witch families, but I doubted there were even any witches in Salem. Besides that, I wasn't sure I liked the casual way Ella was talking about it. As though Penelope deserved what she got just because she might be a witch.

There was a reason 'don't tell anyone' was drilled into me from before I said my first word.

Abigail snorted. "Ridiculous."

"What is?" Ella asked.

Abigail set her cup aside and skewered Ella with a no-nonsense look. "It's ridiculous to think that Penelope was a witch who started the whole thing just because it stopped when she disappeared. Those people. Didn't it occur to them that her wicked husband did away with her?"

"But there's no sign that he didn't love her," Ella protested.

"And who do you think wrote those history books, Ella? He did, that's who. Why would he talk about hating his wife?" Abigail shook her head hard, her wispy grey hair fluttering about her. "No. No, it's just like people to blame the victim for causing everything."

Ella shrugged. "I never thought she was a witch. I bet that it really was wolves. People went running around the countryside and got taken by wolves, or they got lost, or whatever. Winter is harsh, it doesn't need supernatural help. But I don't see why we should jump to Penelope being murdered by her husband, either."

Abigail snorted as she picked up her mug again. "It's because she was the one who owned everything, not him. Not to mention he remarried in a matter of months."

It looked like the two of them were winding up for a good argument. Not that either was a firm believer in what they said. Ella and Abigail liked to have debates. They'd argue over what I thought were silly things, but for them, it was about making themselves see from a new point of view. It was all in good spirits for them.

I didn't want to be caught in the middle of it tonight, though.

"I wonder if this has anything to do with David Blackwood," I wondered aloud.

Ella gave me a funny look. "It can't have anything to do with him. It's just a story about how the festival started. Now we have lights, and people are all out to frighten the wolves away from the town. It's just a coincidence that he disappeared at the same time."

Oh, but there was no such thing as coincidence when magic was concerned. I kept my expression smooth, and Ella started the movie.

My mind kept racing over everything, though, and I couldn't settle. So, when my phone rang, I didn't even mind. I pulled it from my pocket.

"Hello?"

"It's Percival Whitman. You still have my key to the museum," he said. "I need you to meet me there right away."

## 3

# MIDNIGHT WHISPERS

"Don't go," Abigail said.

I stuffed my phone back into my pocket. "I have to go. It sounded important."

And maybe with Percival instead of Liam, I'd be able to get more answers. Liam was too sharp-eyed. With Percival, I might call on David's spirit and better find out what happened. I grabbed my keys with Ella and Abigail following close after me.

"It will do you no good to get mixed up with him," Abigail insisted. "At least call the detective and let him know what's happening."

I frowned at her. "You're talking as though Percival is going to hurt me."

"I never said that. But my bones are creaking, and there's frost out there. It's best to be wary and wise," Abigail said.

Was she trying to give me a hint? I searched her face, unable to read her. She seemed to be genuinely worried. Did she know something that I didn't? I chewed my lower lip. I really felt like I needed to go, but Abigail was right in that it wasn't exactly the smartest thing to do, to race out into the night when there was something out there that was causing trouble.

"I'll go with you," Ella said. She already had her coat on, her expression determined. "I can see on your face that you're going to go, even if you're unsure. So, I'm coming, too, and I'm bringing bear spray."

I smiled gratefully at her. Abigail didn't seem to be assayed but didn't argue with us any further.

"I'll call you in half an hour," I promised her and set the alarm on my phone as proof.

"Be careful, Harper," she warned.

Ella and I headed out. We reached the museum shortly to find all the lights on inside and the door wide open. Percival Whitman's car sat in the parking lot, the engine idling.

"Bear spray out," Ella said, holding the canister ready to spray.

She eyed the surrounding darkness nervously as we made our way to the museum. When I stepped through the door, I gasped. Percival Whitman lay face-down in the center of the room. His hair was matted around a nasty, bleeding injury.

I ran to his side. "Ella, keep a lookout."

She hurried to stand next to us, keeping her back to the wall while she watched the displays nervously. "Do you think they're still here?"

"I don't know."

I touched Percival's skin. He was still warm, so I picked up his hand gently and pressed my fingers to his wrist. His heart pounded. I released a heavy breath of relief.

"He's alive. Call Liam while I check for other injuries."

Ella reached into her pocket one-handed. I thought of the first-aid training I'd gone through and carefully swept my hands beneath Percival's body, checking for further bleeding injuries. With a head injury, I didn't want to move him in case we might damage him further.

"I don't have a signal," Ella said.

The wind howled, slamming the door shut. The windows rattled. Then the wind died, leaving us in an eerie silence—and a bitter cold. My breath puffed out visibly as I went to the door. It was stuck. Ella stood guard near Percival, so I whispered a spell—only for it to bounce off the door and disappear in a puff of smoke.

Nerves swept through me. There *was* magic happening here!

"The furnace isn't kicking on," I said as I lifted my hand to a nearby vent. "It didn't seem to work earlier, either. Let's see if we can start a fire."

"Isn't that dangerous?" Ella asked anxiously.

I shook my head grimly. "We'll freeze if we don't."

She shuddered. It didn't take long to search the small museum. To our relief, no attackers were hiding in the basement or archives. We found an old metal stove and dragged it up to the office space, setting it near Percival. There were also several old clothes and blankets we used to cover him up; he was getting cold, though his heart was still steady.

Neither of us wanted to burn anything important, so we dug into the recycling bins and found scrap paper. I sent Ella to the basement looking for matches, then whispered a fire spell and set our bounty ablaze.

"I found some matches in David's desk," I yelled down to her.

Ella returned, wrapping her arms around herself. "It's so cold."

We both sat near the stove, twisting the paper into tight rolls so they would burn slower. We quickly went through all the recycling. Frost covered the windows and crept over the sills. I didn't like the look of it.

"Still no signal," Ella said, pacing back and forth with her phone in hand.

I looked at my phone. The bars were empty, but the alarm I'd set for Abigail was still ticking down. How long after the allotted time would she wait before she got nervous? I added another twist of paper —and then jumped up as Ella screamed.

She'd put her hand on the windowsill, and the frost crawled up her skin. I raced over to her, but I was too late. The frost crept up over her face, and she collapsed, her eyes rolling to the back of her head.

"Ella!" I cried, catching her. I nearly dropped her, but dragged her closer to the stove.

The frost melted off her, but she remained cold and unconscious. Her breathing was deep and even, though, and her heartbeat was steady. I added more paper to the flames, then held both my hands upward and conjured my flames.

The frost retreated a little, then crept forward again. It spread past the windowsills and under the door, reaching icy fingers toward us.

"Harper Nightshade," a voice whispered.

I jumped and turned. There, on the far wall, a face emerged in the frost. My heart hammered; it was David! His eyes rolled and roved, as though he was in deep pain.

"Who did this?" I cried. "David, who killed you?"

"Beware the wolf in the wind," he whispered, and his face contorted as though each word was painful. "Search the Whitman words. They hold the key."

"Whitman words?" I repeated.

David howled and vanished.

What did he mean? Maybe he left notes? I raced to his desk and extinguished the flames on my hands. I searched through the drawers and finally found an old book. It was worn and delicate, and written by hand. I turned to the first page and read: *This is the journal of Penelope Whitman, 1615.*

Howls rose all around the museum. My head snapped up, and I clutched the journal to my chest. The breath left my lungs. There, in the frost covering the wall, a pair of glowing orange eyes glared at me. A wolf emerged from the frost.

It snarled, eyes locked on me.

The door banged open, and I screamed.

I readied myself to conjure a wind to defend myself with when Liam came in, holding a tazer in one hand. His dark eyes scanned the room before locking on me.

I shook hard as I stood there, my eyes wide. The wolf had disappeared the moment Liam entered. The frost melted at once, leaving only the barest trace on the windows. The temperature rose several degrees.

"Harper, are you okay?" Liam asked as he strode forward.

I swayed on the spot, suddenly exhausted. I braced myself on the desk. "Percival and Ella need the hospital."

"Let's get you out; I'll come back for them." Liam put an arm around my shoulders and helped me to the car, then went back in and carried out first Ella, then Percival. Percival helped to walk himself out;

it seemed he was getting some consciousness back. But as soon as he was in the car, he groaned and fell back to sleep.

When Liam pulled out of the parking lot, I saw a vague canine shape in the shadows of the trees, watching us. But it was gone before I could get a closer look.

"How did you know to come?" I asked as I slumped into my seat.

"Abigail called me," he replied. "You shouldn't have come out here like this, Harper. You could have been hurt."

I shook my head slowly. "If I hadn't, then wouldn't Percival have been killed? Ella and I must have scared off the attacker."

Liam's lips thinned. "The door was locked from the outside. Whoever did this wasn't scared off. I also smelled gasoline around the place. They were planning on burning it down, with the three of you inside."

A shudder raced down my spine. But even so, it made little sense. Why would someone go through that much trouble and also send the frost after us? I held my arms tighter around the book, pressing it into my ribs. The answer was here, somewhere. But I was far too tired to figure it out.

My vision darkened. I was going to pass out. Swallowing hard, I pushed the journal into Liam's lap.

"It holds the key," I told him. But he wouldn't believe David told me, so I added, "The desk was open, this was on the floor. Percival must have interrupted the attacker trying to steal it."

Then the darkness overwhelmed me, and I slumped against the cold window. And the last thing I heard was Liam calling my name.

# 4

# CHILLING REVELATIONS

I woke up warm and cozy in a hospital bed. Liam sat on a chair beside my bed, his eyes closed as he rested his head back against the wall. Surprise flooded through me, followed swiftly by a warmth in my chest. How long had he been sitting here, watching over me?

He stirred as I watched him, and I quickly looked away so he wouldn't know. Liam yawned, stretching his arms over his head. When he focused on me, I smiled up at him.

"You're awake." He grinned at me. "How do you feel?"

"Fine," I answered honestly.

Liam rested a hand on the bed next to mine. "No lingering headache?"

I shook my head. "What about Ella and Percival? Are they okay?"

"Yes. Both of them are still unconscious but they'll be fine. You were all very lucky."

I frowned at his tone. His face was pinched with worry, and I shook my head again, tracing back through my memories. Why would he say that? Was there another attempt at the museum? Or was there something else...?

"Did you find David Blackwood?" I asked him.

"No." His expression grew grave. "What happened? Tell me everything. You kept talking about a wolf all the way to the hospital."

"I was?"

Liam combed his fingers through his hair. "You were delirious, but it sounded important."

I bit my lip. How much could I actually tell him without him thinking I was crazy? But he needed to know everything, didn't he? I couldn't tell him about my magic, but if I told him about everything else... I sighed as I started from when Ella and I arrived and went through detailing everything.

Knowing him and his practicality, he'd come up with an explanation for it.

"Then, after David disappeared, and I found the journal, a wolf stepped through the frost. I knew it was going to kill us all." I shuddered as I remembered those deadly orange eyes. "You broke the door down, and it disappeared."

Liam's brows were lifted almost to his hairline. But he didn't call me crazy. Instead, he nodded slowly. "That explains it."

I chewed my lip again. Did he believe me?

I needn't have worried.

"When I looked through the museum again, I found the furnace was turned on, leaking gas into the building. You three were all suffering carbon monoxide poisoning. You hallucinated the whole thing," he said. His tone was clearly meant to be soothing.

Leaking gas? But we had a fire in that little stove. If we'd been subjected to carbon monoxide, wouldn't the whole place have lit up? No, whoever attacked Percival and locked Ella and me in the museum must have snuck in after we'd left to set the stage.

I couldn't help but flinch as I thought of whoever it was, watching and waiting for us.

Liam leaned forward, his expression worried. "Do you need a doctor?"

"No. It's just scary to think of," I blurted.

A knock came on the door. Abigail stepped through and beamed when she saw I was awake. She carried a thermos in one hand, a tightly wrapped bundle under her elbow. She hurried over to the bed and set them down on my nightstand.

"Oh, my dear! I'm so happy to see that you're alright," she said, hugging me tightly.

"Thank you for calling Liam. We wouldn't have made it out if you hadn't," I told her fervently.

Abigail released me and stepped back. Her smile faltered as she cupped my face in her hands. "Didn't I tell you not to go? Didn't I say Percival Whitman would be up to no good?"

"He was attacked," I protested. "When Ella and I came in, we found him with a nasty blow on the back of his head."

"Did he?" Abigail's eyes widened.

I nodded and then encouraged her to take a seat. "If we hadn't gone, he might have died. But everything worked out this time. I just wish we could have found something that would lead us to David."

Liam stood up. "Speaking of, I should go back to my investigation. Whoever did this has to have left clues at the museum. I need to do a more thorough look."

"But by this time, the attacker would have cleaned up after themselves," I said.

"I had a deputy standing guard."

I nodded, then spied the journal beneath his arm. "Oh! Let me see that. The journal."

Liam held it out to me. "I was going to leave it here, anyway. I don't know what's so special about it, it's just an old journal."

"I told you, I found it on the floor," I said, remembering my lie. "So, someone was interested in it. And it's Penelope Whitman's journal, too."

Abigail's eyes widened but Liam just looked confused. Right, he wasn't part of the discussion about how the Winter Festival got its start. That was definitely something he would not accept. He'd think it was just a coincidence, and I'd pushed my luck too much already.

I turned the book over in my hands, studying it. David had led me to it for a reason. But why?

A strange lump in the binding caught my eye. I pressed my fingers over it, to find something hard in a strange shape. Carefully, I pressed the flaps of the book backward, making the binding bend slightly. A key fell out of the spine, landing in my lap.

"What's that?" Abigail asked, leaning forward.

"It looks new." I studied it. "Maybe for a safe? David must have put it in there... maybe this is what the attacker was looking for?"

I reached for it, but Liam caught my wrist. "There might be prints."

He put on a glove and carefully picked it up, dropping it into a small plastic baggy. Then he sealed it and tucked the key into his jacket.

"Do you think it will help?" I asked him.

"I don't know. With any luck, it will. We have no prints to go on, yet."

He gave me a searching look. Not suspicious, but like he knew there was something more about this whole situation than I was letting on. I longed to know exactly what he was thinking. If he didn't suspect me as the attacker, what did he think I knew? Was he suspicious about why I was involved in the case?

Or was there something else? Had I been too reckless, telling him about what I saw in the museum?

"I'll check on you later," Liam told me.

"Thanks." I blushed. It was sweet that he'd do that for me when our relationship thus far hadn't exactly been friendly.

But Liam wasn't a regular sort of person. He genuinely cared about others. He was only looking out for me because he felt like he needed to protect everyone in town, and I was one of the few unfortunates who had been in danger lately. He would check in on Ella and Percival too, I was sure.

Once he was gone, Abigail pulled a tin of cookies from the bundle she brought. "These are for you. They'll get you on your feet in no time."

"Thanks," I said, grinning at her.

"I'm going to go sit with Ella for a bit. The poor thing hasn't woken up yet," Abigail said. She patted my hand. "I'll be right across the hall."

I nodded once at her and settled down to read. I felt fine, but it'd probably be good to give myself a bit more time. Besides, David told me to read the Whitman words. There had to be a clue in here, besides the key.

I opened the book and read the first line again. There was something off about Penelope's name. It seemed smudged somehow. I frowned at it for a while before I kept reading. I skimmed the first few pages until a name caught my eye.

*My brother, Jeremiah Blackwood, disappeared today. They say there were wolf tracks around his homestead. There haven't been wolves in the area for years now. I worry that this is linked to my cousin's death last year, but nobody will listen to me. It's just a coincidence, they say.*

Penelope was a Blackwood by birth? So, she must be distantly related to David. I turned the page and my eyes widened.

*Howard Whitman came to ask for my hand again today. He's always asking in secret and begs me not to tell anyone. He makes me feel uneasy. His mother has invited me to come stay in their townhouse since Papa was killed by the wolves. I don't want to live with the Whitmans. I'll take my chances with the frost. Howard is just as cold and I swear I have seen him walking with wolves at night.*

My heart pounded harder as I kept reading. When did she change her mind? Or was there another Whitman that she married? As I read, the air left my lungs. Every person who disappeared were relatives of Penelope.

And all their land, which totaled more than half of the properties in and around Moonhaven, all ended up going to her.

So that's how the Whitmans ended up owning the land. Whichever Whitman Penelope married, inherited it as her widower.

Only...

I turned back to the first page again.

Only, if she was rejecting Howard Whitman's proposals later on, why was her name Whitman on the first page?

It all clicked at once why her name looked smudged. Because someone had scrubbed out what she actually wrote and placed the Whitman name over it. My hand pressed to my mouth as I realized what this meant. Penelope Blackwood never married a Whitman.

Which meant all the Blackwood land should have belonged to David, not Percival.

## 5

# FESTIVAL OF FEARS

Abigail was still with Ella but didn't know where Percival's room was. When I went to the nurse's station, they told me he had checked himself out of the hospital an hour ago. Blood rushed in my ears as the pieces kept falling into place.

I dashed to my car and called Liam. If anyone could help me figure this out and stop Percival, it was him.

"Liam," I blurted as soon as he answered. "It was Percival Whitman. It was him all this time. David Blackwood uncovered proof that the Whitmans stole the Blackwood land."

"You might be onto something," Liam replied. "I'm at the museum now. That key you found didn't have any prints, but it unlocked a safe here. It's full of documents and property deeds in the Blackwood and Whitman names. David must have spent months researching this."

I started my car and pulled out of the hospital parking lot. Where would Percival have gone?

"David must have confronted him about it. Maybe he was giving Percival a chance to do the right thing, or maybe just giving him the heads up that he'd be revealing all of it to the public," I said as I drove toward Main Street. "Percival had a key to the museum. He could have easily snuck in and attacked David."

And if his ancestor had magic wolves, it followed to reason that Percival was a wolf, too.

There was the sound of a metal door closing and Liam's breathing became harder, like he was rushing up a set of stairs. "Where are you?"

"Looking for him," I said.

"Get back to the hospital. Don't you see what this means? He wasn't unconscious in the museum when Ella and you showed up. He set the scene to make it look like he'd been attacked," Liam said, sounding urgent. "He must have set it all up to lure you in. But he didn't know about the gas leak, which knocked him out before he could lock you and Ella into the museum and light it on fire."

Not exactly... he used his ancestral magic to bring the frost and the wolves in, then must have gone back to set the furnace leaking. Nobody would suspect him when he was unconscious in the hospital, after all. He'd put it all together perfectly. The one thing he hadn't expected was that Liam would arrive right in time to stop it.

He used the same tactics as his ancestor, the one who had forged a marriage to Penelope and then killed her to steal all of her land. But what was his plan? If it was just about preventing David from telling the truth about what happened four hundred years ago, he wouldn't have continued all of this... which meant he had other plans.

The festival? Was he planning to use the energy of everyone coming together to do something?

Howard Whitman, all those years ago, attacked many, many people. He put the blame on Penelope to divert suspicion even though he was the one who would profit... Percival had to be planning something similar. He was going to attack more victims to muddy the waters and make it seem like he wasn't part of it at all.

"Harper," Liam said urgently. "Go back to the hospital. Tell them what's happening. He'll go after you again."

I tightened my hands on the wheel. "If he does, he won't know what hit him."

The phone went dead. My heart jumped to my throat as I twisted to stare at it. At first, I thought we were wrong and Percival had gone after Liam—then I realized the signal bars were empty.

My car skidded and I pumped the brakes, my breath exhaling in puffs of white. When I finally stopped, I threw open the door. The road was slick with frost. I scrambled out of the car and leaped onto the sidewalk.

The frost crept up over my car and toward the center of town. A chill ran down my spine—no, it wasn't just about me and Ella in the museum. That was to set himself up as a victim. But this? This was so much bigger... He would not have a single attacker anymore.

It was the wolves. Percival Whitman was bringing the wolves to town. He was going to have a bloodbath, so nobody would even think about what had happened. He must have changed his plans the moment I gave Liam Penelope's journal, knowing that we'd figure out what had happened so far.

Fog rose from the frost. A figure appeared in the fog, moving away from me. My blood rushed in my ears as I took up the chase, following him. I whispered a spell, bringing my guiding winds up. It tugged me this way and that until I was out of town and heading into the forest.

"Tenacious, aren't you?" Percival purred from behind me.

I whirled, then shied back. He held a glowing, icy orb in his hands. Two monster wolves flanked him on either side, their orange eyes focused on me while their tails swished. I glanced around quickly, but it seemed like those two wolves were the only ones there.

"Surprised, Harper?" Percival cooed. "This is far from what you expected, isn't it? Too bad you won't have any answers before you die. It'll be the tragic mystery of Moonhaven, a town slaughtered by wolves who disappeared without a trace."

He laughed and pointed at me. The two wolves sprang forward silently.

I threw my hands out, palms toward them. I shouted an incantation and fire burned from my skin. It arced through the air and melted the first wolf. The second dodged and retreated, growling. Its hair stood on end.

Percival's eyes widened. "Impossible!"

"Guess you're not the only witch in town," I spat at him. I crouched, drawing my flames closer around me. "I understand more about what you've done here than you know. Unfortunately for you, David told me enough."

Percival's face twisted. "You didn't even know him!"

"I didn't need to. I'm a Nightshade. Our specialties are fire and death," I told him, smirking.

The second wolf attacked suddenly. I dodged the attack, whipping my flames around. They whipped against the wolf, and it vanished in sparkles of water vapor that fluttered toward the ground. I straightened and faced Percival again.

"We know the truth now. Your plan won't work. We know you're the one who attacked David. If you send your wolves into town, the only thing that'll happen is that you'll be guilty of more murders."

Percival laughed, an arrogant, raucous sound. "Oh, but if everyone dies, then it doesn't matter who knows, does it?"

He charged me. I sent my flames at him but a burst of ice cracked through the air. Fire and ice met and canceled each other out. Then Percival threw his glowing orb aside and slammed into me. The breath was knocked out of me, my flames dying at once. He wrapped his hands around my throat and squeezed.

I clawed at his hands, but it did no good. I couldn't even summon my flames again.

"I will not lose everything!" he yelled as he tightened his grip. "David Blackwood should have minded his own business! This town belongs to me. I don't care if I have to kill everyone in it! There will be more people. I'll always be able to turn a profit."

I grabbed a handful of snow and threw it into his face. His head jerked back, and I punched forward, jabbing my thumb into his eye.

Percival howled. His grip on me loosened. I shoved at him, making him topple into the snow. I turned, trying to crawl away while fighting to re-inflate my lungs. My throat burned. I couldn't get air in except in noisy gasps.

"Oh, no you don't," Percival shouted. He grabbed my legs and pulled me back.

He was going to kill me. I wheezed, trying to bring my flames forward. He grabbed my wrist and flipped me back onto my back. The fury and hatred in his eyes sent ice through my blood. The frost swirled nearby and a wolf appeared, crouched in the snow.

A sudden crack filled the air. Percival's eyes widened as he toppled over, both of his hands cradling his skull. Abigail stood behind him, her thermos in hand. She reached for me, her eyes wild with fright.

"Come on, let's get you out of—"

The wolf howled and jumped at her, knocking her over. I let out a hoarse shout as I pulled my flames up and shot them at the wolf. It disappeared, but Abigail didn't move, her eyes shut. A trickle of blood ran down her forehead.

Percival laughed as he staggered back to his feet. "Looks like she was knocked out by her own thermos. No matter. I'll deal with you first and then the old woman. Say goodbye, Harper Nightshade."

## 6

# A WARM WINTER'S NIGHT

I inched backward as my flames fizzled out. Percival's eyes were blazing as he stalked toward me like one of his wolves.

Just as I was dredging up the last of my strength, a flurry of footsteps hailed the approach of another person. We both turned. Liam burst through the trees and smashed into Percival. They went flying, and I cried out through my bruised throat. They rolled through the snow, grappling with each other.

I crawled to Abigail. Her skin was grey and cold, but she was breathing. I grabbed the thermos, surprised at the weight of it, and turned, ready to hurl it toward Percival.

Liam was on top, pinning him to the ground. Percival's face pressed into the snow as he weakly thrashed. I waited, my heart in my throat, for further wolves to appear. They didn't. Liam was currently cuffing Percival's hands behind his back. All around us, the frost melted.

The glowing orb he'd had before lay nearby, cracked down the middle. Abigail must have broken it when she fell... and with it, Percival lost his ability to use the magic inside. It was the only explanation I could come up with.

I checked Abigail's head, finding that she was bleeding pretty badly. I pulled off my jacket and put it over her.

How was I going to explain any of this to anyone?

I'll figure it out later. Sirens pierced the night as Liam dragged Percival to his feet. He tilted his head and nodded in satisfaction.

"I'm going to get this slimeball to the cruiser and come back for you; the ambulance will be here soon."

"Thanks," I murmured shakily. "Hurry, I don't enjoy being out here by myself."

Liam's gaze lingered on mine. He opened his mouth as though to say something... then closed it and shoved Percival through the trees. I tucked my jacket tighter around Abigail, hoping that she'd be okay. She saved my life, again. I didn't know what I'd do if it ended up costing her everything.

"Please be okay," I whispered to her, wishing that healing was among my skills. "Please, Abigail. Please be okay."

⋯⋯⋯

Ella squeezed my hands as we sat in the hospital waiting room. She had, apparently, woken suddenly only minutes before we brought Abigail in. From the sounds of it, her waking coincided perfectly with when my showdown with Percival happened.

"I can't wait any longer," she said, standing. "I'm going to—Doctor Rika. Is Abigail okay?"

She raced forward as Moonhaven's only resident doctor, Rika Furukawa, entered the waiting room. We were lucky to have transit doctors come through, but everyone knew Doctor Rika. She smiled at Ella. I hurried to join them. A smile was a good sign, right?

"She's awake and responding well to all our tests. I believe she may have a mild concussion, so I want to keep her under supervision for a while longer. She's asking about both of you."

The hospital bay doors opened. A handful of paramedics came in with Liam following them. They pushed a stretcher. Ella grabbed my arm as we stepped to one side.

"Middle-aged male in a hypothermic state," one paramedic said.

"Get him to room four. Betsy, I'm going to need help," Rika said, growing professional at once.

She hurried after the paramedics while Liam stopped next to Ella and me. I gasped as the man was wheeled past. His skin was ashy and his eyes closed, but I recognized that face.

Ella yanked at my arm in her excitement. "David Blackwood! He's alive?"

"When I took Percival to the station for booking, I found I had an anonymous note on my desk, telling me where to find him. He was tied up in an old wolf's den. He's lucky we've been having warmer nights lately," Liam said, running his hand through his short hair distractedly. "Being as deep as he was in the ground saved his life. A few more hours with the frost tonight..."

I let out a shaky breath and squeezed Ella's hand. "Why don't you go tell Abigail the news? She'll want to know he's okay."

"Abigail's awake?" Liam asked eagerly.

"Yeah."

He looked dead on his feet, so I sent him to sit down and got a coffee for him. He accepted it gratefully and took a long sip.

"There's still a lot that doesn't add up. Who left that note? Why would they do that, rather bring David back themselves?" Liam said. He looked up at me, searching, as though he expected I was the one who left it.

"I don't know anything about that." But I had a suspicion.

That icy ball that Percival had could have been a connector. Something that was using David's life force to enhance Percival's magic. It made sense why the apparitions of David I saw were so strange. He hadn't acted like a spirit, because he wasn't dead.

David himself might have left that note when Percival's power over him broke.

"I'm glad that Abigail is okay," Liam murmured at last. "And Percival is locked up. I think he must have been heading into the forest to finish David off when you interrupted him, which you shouldn't have done. You could have been killed."

His gaze flitted over the bruises on my neck.

"I had to," I told him.

Liam took another sip of coffee. "I guess you did, didn't you? I'm just glad you're okay."

"I'm glad you're okay, too," I said, blushing. We sat in a comfortable silence. I had a feeling that our relationship would not be quite so frosty from here on out.

The End
Did you enjoy Whispers in the Winter Frost?
Please consider rating it on <u>Amazon</u>, <u>Goodreads</u>, or <u>Bookbub</u>.
Reviews help me reach new readers.
Read Valentine Vendetta, the next story in the Mystic Moonhaven Mysteries.

Have you read the *Jane and Kennedy Daniels Mysteries*, the *Annie Archer Paranormal Mysteries*, the *Wilma Wade Holiday Mysteries,* the *Mike and Maddie Mysteries* or the *Pine Grove Mysteries?*

# 1

## HEARTS AND SHADOWS

The first day of my first job at the tender age of thirteen was on February fourteenth. Valentine's Day. The wretched experience left me drained and bitter. I vowed from that day forward, I would never work another Valentine's Day again. It didn't matter if I was dating or not—and most of the days since, it was the 'not.'

Which was why, now that I owned my bookstore in the beautiful little town of Moonhaven, I had a giant 'Closed for Valentine's' sign on my front door and all the blinds drawn. I was cheating a little, though. I'd bought a few cases of used books the day before, so I was processing the titles with a glass of strawberry-rhubarb juice while I listened to Loreena McKennitt.

I'd only recently started selling used books in my shop. Not because I was suffering for it, but I'd realized that I was pricing out a good portion of Moonhaven by selling only new books.

Books should be accessible to everyone. Everything that I didn't have a place for, I'd donate to the library's book sale.

I hummed along with the music as I picked out the book that made me buy this batch. It was an ancient edition of Shakespeare's Sonnets, kept in prime condition. I gingerly opened the book, holding my breath as I did so. It was perfect.

I opened it up, and a paper dropped out, floating across the room.

Setting the book aside, I waved my hand and muttered a spell. My retrieval wind blew from my fingertips and raced across the room. It lifted the paper back up and carried it, swirling and fluttering, back to me. I plucked it from the air and laid it down on the table.

The paper had jagged lines, like someone had tried to cut it down to size with a shaking hand. "My heart" was written in a beautiful script on the front. I opened it up to find a sonnet written in the centerfold.

*Your sunlight casts o'er the long road so bleak*
*Lifting both heart and soul of the weary one*
*A sadness now betrayed by one so meek*
*My life, my love, my heart, my joy, my sun*

*Love, each moment is etched deep in my soul*
*My life, my love, my heart, my joy, my sun*
*I thought death had left my heart black as coal*
*What is love? What is light? 'Tis you, dear one*

*At dawn, I cast my face toward the light*
*Your light, my love, still gives me strength to move*
*Where is your hand that I may hold it tight?*
*Oh, let me see you! Let my love so prove*
*Me I say, me I say, yet I am night*
*Go, my love. Go, my heart. Be still my light*

Tears pricked my eyes. Poetry always got me, but this felt like a love letter and a poem of despair all wrapped together. No, I couldn't say it was great poetry, but I could still feel the passion with which it was written.

There was something off about it though. I didn't know enough about the details of sonnets to figure out what it was. Probably it was just that the writer wasn't a great poet, despite being able to touch me.

I studied the flourish of the author's name. Adam Carter.

I lowered the page, my eyes widening. Adam Carter was the victim of a single-car accident outside of Moonhaven just last week. From the way it was addressed, I had to think that he had meant to deliver this love letter sonnet to whoever 'my heart' was.

He couldn't do it anymore, but that didn't mean it could never be delivered. I'd find out who he was in love with and deliver the letter myself! How hard could it be?

I grabbed my glass of juice and downed it, then packed away the books other than the Shakespeare sonnets. After carefully flipping through the pages, I discovered an envelope in one spot. It had a stamp on it and Adam's address in the top left corner, but the name and address that it was meant to be sent to was smudged.

Opening the envelope, I found another copy of the same poem, typed neatly, and signed the same as the first. This one had crisp edges, though, and was printed onto a floral cardstock.

I still had the contact information of the person who sold me these books, Angela Brae, so I grabbed my phone and called her up.

"Hi, Angela, this is Harper Nightshade," I said when she answered. "I was just wondering if you could tell me more about this book of Shakespeare's Sonnets. I found a letter in it I want to deliver to the intended recipient."

"I don't know anything about that," Angela answered.

"Do you remember where the book came from?"

Angela hummed. "Now let me see. Most of those were collected at estate sales. The Shakespeare one I actually found in a dumpster. I wasn't looking, mind, I just opened it to throw something away and there was that book right on the top. I couldn't leave such a beautiful thing there."

"What dumpster?" I asked eagerly.

"The one behind the grocery store."

My heart sank. That didn't give me any clues at all. Why would anyone throw out this beautiful book in the first place?

"Sorry I can't be more useful," Angela said.

"It's okay. Thanks."

I hung up and hurried to my recycling bin, where I'd put the news-paper. I quickly found Adam's obituary. Nothing stood out in it, either, other than he didn't have any family in town... which meant that the best bet I had in finding information was Ella's Wheel.

My best friend Ella ran a coffee shop across the road. If anyone knew who Adam was in love with, it would be her. She knew every-thing—real and imagined—that went on in Moonhaven.

I shot her a quick text.

> When's your break? I want to chat

The answer was quick.

> An hour. Bring new socks.

I laughed as I tucked my phone away. With an hour to kill, I headed to the B&B where I had been living for the past year. When I first arrived in Moonhaven, grieving the loss of my parents, the kindly owner, Abigail, took me under her wing. It was like living with my grandmother.

"You're back early," Abigail noted when I came in.

"Yeah, I'm going to meet Ella in an hour and she needs fresh socks," I explained. I stepped into the kitchen with her and went to the sink, which was loaded with dirty dishes. I washed them up.

"You don't have to do that," Abigail said.

I shrugged. "You always make such good food for me, and I have time to kill yet."

Abigail smiled her gratitude as she continued to layer strips of bread together. It looked like she was making French sweetbread. One of my favorite goodies. "Anything interesting happen?"

"I found a love letter. Or a poem," I said. "It's signed Adam Carter. I don't know who it was for, so that's why I'm meeting with Ella. I want to deliver it since he wasn't able to."

Abigail clucked her tongue as she shook her head. "Ah, poor Adam. He didn't deserve what happened to him. But are you certain this is a wise idea, Harper?"

"Why not?" I asked, frowning.

Abigail was quiet for a moment. She covered up the bread with a tea towel and turned to me, wiping the flour dust from her hands. "I think you should involve Detective Liam in your quest here. It's better if you stay safe."

I stared at her, confused. What did she mean by that? "Why wouldn't it be safe? I'm just delivering a letter to someone he loved."

"Because I don't think it's that simple. For that matter, I don't believe that his death was an accident at all. Something happened with that crash. It was on purpose." Her mouth was set into a grim line as a haunted look came into her eyes.

"What makes you say that?"

"Oh... it's complicated." Abigail waved a hand, then strode over to rinse off her hands and put away the dishes I'd already washed. "And besides that, it will be good for you and Liam to spend more time together, anyway. You two worked so well together during the Winter Festival."

I narrowed my eyes at her as I continued to wash the dishes. Was this her way of trying to set us up? Not in the romantic sense, but Abigail always seemed to be worried about my social life. While she was always glad to have Ella over, I got the sense that she thought I should make more friends in town.

I had lots of acquaintances, but not as many people I'd call on if I needed help. I supposed she was right.

In this case, though, I didn't see any reason to involve Liam. There wasn't anything in the newspaper or rumor mill about Adam's death being anything but a tragic accident. Liam must be busy, being the only detective in Moonhaven. He investigated everything from tipped mailboxes to break-ins.

On the other hand, I did want to spend more time with him...

"I'll see if he can meet Ella and me," I decided aloud for Abigail's sake. "At the very least, he'll be able to reach out to Adam's family to see if they know who 'my heart' is."

Abigail smiled, but it quickly faded. "Just be careful, Harper. Cupid's arrow can bleed the heart dry as well."

What did that mean? I gave her a puzzled look, but she didn't seem interested in continuing the conversation.

I finished washing up the dishes and kissed her cheek. "I'll see you later."

I headed into my room and grabbed a pair of socks for Ella, then pulled out my phone. I hesitated as I pulled up my text thread with Liam.

Ah, it wouldn't hurt.

> Can you meet me at the coffee shop in half an hour? I found something that belonged to Adam Carter and want to talk to you and Ella about it.

I shoved the socks into my pocket and sat on my bed, watching my phone. My cheeks warmed as I realized what this would look like. Me, sitting here waiting for a text from a boy. But it wasn't like that. This was me reaching out to make friends and hopefully get a little help to solve a mystery.

> I'll be there.

I bit my lip, hiding a grin from myself. Yes! This should end up being a fun mystery to solve, after all.

# 2

## BITTER SWEETHEARTS

The cozy coffee shop was warm and lively. The decorations were all pinks and reds, with hearts dripping off every available surface. It suited Ella's personality to a T, and I loved it. Oh, I hated working on Valentine's Day, but I didn't hate the day itself.

I was already sitting in a booth, the letter and its original handwritten copy tucked into the envelope in front of me. A cheerful chime of bells announced Liam's arrival. He stepped into the shop dressed in a casual flannel jacket. A light dusting of snow covered him, and he shook it off before he headed to my booth.

There, he hung up his jacket next to mine and grinned as he took the seat opposite me. "I'm glad you messaged me. So what is this letter about?"

"Move over," Ella ordered from next to him.

I jumped. I'd been so caught up in Liam that I hadn't realized she had come over. She slid two mugs of coffee onto the table, one to me and one to him. Liam scooted over and she plopped down next to him.

"There you go, both of you with your favorite coffees," Ella said, leaning her elbows against the table. "If I wasn't so wired, I'd have one myself."

"Thanks, Ella," I said, bringing my coffee to my face. The delicious aroma made me close my eyes.

What I wanted to know was how Ella knew Liam's order by heart, too. I was her best friend, so that made sense... On the other hand, Ella could probably tell me all of her regular customers' favorite drink. She was like that. She was the best friend of half the people in Moonhaven.

"Well, what's this letter?" Ella demanded.

I opened my eyes again and slid the envelope over. "I found this in a Shakespeare book. The person I got it from found it in the dumpster behind the grocery store."

Liam pulled the letter out and read it, with Ella peering over his shoulder. When they were done, Ella pressed both her hands to her heart.

"That's beautiful."

"It's bleak," Liam replied. He shook his head. "I don't know what he's trying to say here, whether she improves his life or he makes her life worse. Poetry isn't the way to do these things. A couple should have a discussion about what they want. Not write confusing, florid words to express themselves."

Ella rolled her eyes, looking amused.

I was reminded of the frosty way things used to be between Liam and me. Our relationship had warmed up, but he had such a pragmatic approach to everything that sometimes it still confused me.

"Don't you think there's room for romance, too?" I asked him. "Writing poems and having sweet gestures doesn't mean that there are no talks about what one or both of the parties in the relationship want."

Liam hummed and sipped his coffee. "I suppose you're right. There's something to be said about both approaches. Just so long as everyone in the relationship knows how to communicate their wants and needs."

"Of course. It also means that they have to accept that communication, too. It's not all about talking, it's about listening, too," I pointed out.

Liam smirked at me. "So, what were you hoping to do with this letter?"

"Find out who it was meant for and deliver it."

Ella pulled out her phone. "Can I take a picture?"

I nodded at her.

Liam leaned back in his seat as Ella focused her phone on it. "What makes you think it was meant to be delivered?"

"The envelope is addressed."

Liam turned the envelope around so he could study it. "I'll give you that. On the other hand—"

"No, I don't want to hear arguments or to know that there are other explanations," I interrupted, raising my hand at him. "I know that there are plenty of reasons for this other than him wanting to deliver this message, but my gut says that he wrote it for someone and he wanted them to have it."

Liam's expression remained the same, but I could see the doubt in his eyes.

"Look, what I need from you is to contact his family and see if they might know if he was dating someone. Maybe it was a long-distance relationship," I said.

Ella tucked her phone back into her pocket. "Or maybe it was a local one. Adam used to come into the shop here every Wednesday with the girl who works at the automobile shop. Sophie, I think her name is. They came for months and then about three months ago they abruptly stopped coming."

I'd never heard of Sophie before. I only took my car up to the dealership where I'd bought it for it to be serviced.

"What's Sophie like?" I asked.

"Quiet. She keeps to herself more or less," Ella said, shrugging.

Liam's shoulders grew rigid as he drummed his fingers on the table. I thought about how Abigail claimed that the car accident that killed Adam wasn't an accident at all. If anyone could tinker with a vehicle and cause it to crash, it was someone who worked with cars as their living.

Judging from the way Liam reacted to this news, I couldn't help but think maybe Abigail was right. He certainly seemed to be deep in thought about something.

I focused my attention back on Ella. "Do you know why Adam and Sophie stopped coming around?"

She shook her head.

"Did they have a fight? Did they break up?"

"I don't know. Like I said, Sophie is very quiet," Ella said with a sigh. "And Adam wasn't ever one to share, either. I'm not even sure that they were a couple in the first place. Their talks were very intimate, but not romantic. At least, not to the outward eye."

I sighed.

Liam finished his coffee. "It won't hurt to stop by her place and see if she knows anything. If this letter is for her, maybe Adam had unrequited feelings for her."

"True," Ella agreed.

"We'll take my car," I said, standing. "Oh... do you have her address?"

Ella smirked and pulled her phone out again. "Luckily for you, I do. There. Sent."

I nodded in thanks and grabbed my jacket. Liam was a little slower than I was and I tapped my toes in impatience as he pulled on his jacket. He glanced at my foot and I stopped, blushing. But he only shot me a grin and started for the door while he put his jacket on.

As I drove toward the address Ella had shared, I glanced at Liam from the corner of my eye. He seemed pensive.

"I know a love letter isn't exactly your cup of tea," I said. "But Abigail told me I should bring you along. She says that Adam's death wasn't an accident."

Liam's head whipped toward me. "Why would she say that?"

"I don't know. Was it?"

"I'm investigating," he said cagily.

That meant that it wasn't an accident. "He was murdered?"

Liam winced, then sighed. "His brake lines were cut. I have told no one, though, so how can Abigail possibly have guessed?"

"Abigail's a dedicated people-watcher. I only started thinking she was right when we were in the diner and you tensed up." I shrugged apologetically at him. "At a guess, she saw something in how you reacted some time while she was talking to you and ran with it."

Liam groaned as he ran his hand through his short, dark hair. "That sounds about right, doesn't it? She seems to know everything that happens in town."

"She's lived in Moonhaven all her life. I bet she knows secrets about this town that everyone else has forgotten."

"She certainly always has an answer for the strange events that happen around here."

My hands tightened on the steering wheel, and I fought to keep the shock off my face. What sort of strange things was he talking about? I thought he'd accepted all the reasonable, non-magic explanations as to what happened at the Winter Festival.

I couldn't study him the way I wanted to. I needed to keep my focus on the road; even if I didn't, he had turned his face away from me so I could only see the ridge of his firm jaw. I stayed quiet, worried that anything I'd say would give too much of myself away.

The one vital rule to being a witch was never to tell anyone. Both of my parents were witches, and I'd been born before they ended up figuring out that the other one had magic. And that was only because I'd caught a fever that might have killed me if they hadn't both used healing spells on me.

After everything that had happened to our ancestors, secrecy was the only thing keeping us safe. Even though the world was changing and getting better, it was still the one thing no witch would risk. Even if Liam was grounded, and I doubted he'd believe in magic if I showed it to him, I still couldn't risk it.

Luckily, we were at Sophie's address. I parked and we headed up her driveway. Liam knocked firmly and a couple minutes later, the door opened to reveal a muscular young woman with long hair and steely eyes.

"Detective Ashford," she said in surprise. "What are you doing here? If there's something wrong with the cruiser—"

"Nothing like that," Liam interrupted. He smiled warmly at her. "This is Harper Nightshade. She recently found a letter in a book from Adam Carter. We thought it might be for you."

Sophie's eyes widened. Silently, she stepped back to invite us in. "Victor," she called.

I faltered. Victor? Who was Victor? Ella hadn't mentioned him.

Sophie led us into the living room and sank into a chair. A minute later, a handsome man with pale eyes came into the room, a furrow between his brows. "What's going on?"

"The detective and his friend have a letter to me from Adam," Sophie said, reaching for Victor's hand. She focused on Liam and me again. "This is my husband, Victor."

My eyes widened as Liam and I sat on the couch. Married? It seemed like the letter wasn't so straightforward after all. Had I just stumbled into a love triangle?

## 3

# ROSES ARE RED, VIOLETS ARE BLUE, SOMEONE IS LYING, BUT WHO?

I wasn't sure if I should hand the letter over to Sophie while her husband was sitting right there. I did, because that's why we were there. If there was something between Sophie and Adam, then either Victor already knew about it or he deserved to know. The whole situation made me feel uncomfortable.

Sophie read the sonnet, and her lip trembled. Tears leaked down her face and she leaned into Victor's side. He wrapped his arms around her, his gaze skimming first over the letter, then back to peer at Liam and me suspiciously.

"The name and address on the envelope are smudged, so we couldn't be sure who it was meant for," I hedged.

Sophie shook her head, not looking at us. "It's for me. He used to write me sonnets and always called me his light."

Victor rubbed her back. "I don't mean to be rude, but why is this a police matter? Why should a detective be involved in delivering a letter?"

His suspicion increased as he narrowed his eyes at Liam. His arms around Sophie were so protective that it made me feel bad for suspecting her—and now him—as part of the reason why Adam died. Liam shifted in his seat as he cleared his throat.

"This isn't exactly a police matter," he started.

I grabbed his hand and squeezed it in both of mine. "Actually, I asked him to come along. I was nervous about meeting with strangers, and I also wasn't sure how the letter would be received. Especially after the recent tragedy. I wanted moral support."

I'm not sure who was more surprised, me or him. The way I was holding his hand and what I said made it sound like we were a couple. I snuck a look at him; the only sign that he was surprised was a slight widening in his blue eyes.

He shifted his hand in mine, twining our fingers together. His hand was so warm in mine that I pulled him closer unconsciously.

"Although it doesn't appear that the letter was mailed, it is technically protected property. I wouldn't want there to be any legal misunderstandings," he explained. "But that's all there is to it. I'm not here in my capacity as a detective."

I smiled at him, and he smiled back. I wasn't sure that was entirely right; he was here in part because Adam was murdered. But then, I suppose he wasn't here because he was a detective, but because I asked him.

Sophie pulled away from Victor and dried her eyes. "I suppose this must look strange to you, delivering a love letter to a married woman. Adam and I dated our senior year in high school. He moved to the city for school and it proved to be too difficult, so we broke up."

Victor kissed her temple.

"We kept in touch, but we both agreed it was best if we didn't try to be a couple," Sophie continued. "When he moved back to town, he thought we would pick up where we left off. I told him clearly that my feelings had changed. I wasn't interested in a romantic relationship. He was so upset but begged me to stay friends. I wanted to be friends, so I agreed. Looking back, I don't know if I led him on or not."

"He never accepted you at your word. That's not your fault," Victor told her.

She sighed. "I had to cut all communication with him about three months ago. He was acting erratic. I was afraid he'd started on drugs or something."

Liam leaned forward, his hand still in mine. "I'm sorry. That sounds rough. Was he threatening you at all?"

"No. Nothing like that. It was the letters." Sophie shook her head as she smoothed the letter I'd just delivered. "He kept leaving me all these poems. When I stopped talking to him, he stopped sending them."

She looked so heartbroken and guilty that I had to look away. I had luckily never been in a situation where I was faced with a friend who hoped for more. I could imagine just how painful it all would be, though.

As I sighed though, I caught sight of a book sitting on a stand beside a reading chair. It was a copy of Shakespeare's Tragedies, hidden beneath a pile of magazines. And sticking out from the edge was a piece of stationery with the same design as in the letter I just delivered.

"My leg is cramping up. Do you mind if I walk it off?" I asked, standing.

"No, go ahead," Sophie said, sniffling.

I paced, keeping one leg stiff as I did so.

"Do you know what triggered his behavior?" Liam asked.

I was impressed by how easily he led the conversation. With just these simple questions, we were getting a much better picture of what happened.

"I happened," Victor said bleakly. "Sophie and I met about a year ago. We didn't start dating right away, but we both felt the connection."

"I thought Adam had accepted that we were friends, nothing more." Sophie wiped her eyes again. "I really thought that we were at a good place. But as soon as Victor and I dated, he acted crazy. It was like he became a different person entirely."

With Sophie and Victor's attention still on Liam, I slid the Shakespeare into my purse.

"I don't suppose you know where he was or what he was doing the day he died?" Liam asked.

I came back to the couch and sat back down, taking his hand. I tried to look nonchalant as I did so.

Victor sighed. "Sophie and I were at a bar the day of the crash. We saw him there, drunk as anything. It's tragic what happened, don't get me wrong. But it was a tragedy of his own making. He never should have been driving in that condition."

"Especially on these roads," Sophie murmured. She passed a weary hand over her face. "He never took good care of his vehicle. I'd been trying to get him to get winter tires for months now. The all-weather ones just don't work for our winter conditions. But I'd tried to teach him how to take care of his vehicle in the past and he was never interested."

Victor squeezed her hands. "It's not your fault, Sophie. He's responsible for himself."

"Why would you think it was your fault?" I asked, startled to hear such a declaration.

"Because I knew he was in love with me. Maybe I didn't put down firm enough boundaries. Maybe I—"

Victor shook his head, interrupting Sophie as he squeezed her hands. "No. It's not your fault. He's the one who kept pursuing you even after you told him you didn't share his feelings. I know it hurts, my love, but it's not your fault."

Liam sighed. "I don't think we'll ever know why he drank and drove that day."

"But we do know," Sophie insisted. "It's because—"

"Sophie," Victor said, shaking his head.

I looked between the two of them, leaning forward as I did so. What was going on? It seemed like he was trying to warn her off of saying something. But what? And why?

"What?" Sophie snapped at him. "It'll get out soon enough." She turned back to us. "Victor and I eloped the day of Adam's death. We were at the bar celebrating. He knew we were dating, but like I said, I hadn't seen him in three months. I guess he saw our rings and..."

Her shoulders slumped as she ran her fingers down the letter. "And I guess he was still in love with me."

Liam stood, tugging me to my feet with him. "We're very sorry for taking up your time. I hope we haven't caused you more pain."

"I'm sorry for your loss," I murmured.

We left together, only releasing one another's hands when we got into the car. Once we were driving away, Liam rolled his shoulders. Tension crept into the way he held himself and I shot him sidelong glances as I drove back toward the coffee shop.

"Adam Carter had no alcohol in his system," Liam finally said. "He was taking a few prescription medications, but that doesn't explain his cut brakes."

"I found something," I blurted.

Liam frowned at me.

"It's in my purse. I saw they had a copy of Shakespeare, which matches the book I found the letter in."

"In your purse?" Liam repeated. He straightened. "You mean you stole their property?"

Ah. Yes. "Well... technically, I suppose."

Liam slumped back again. "And admitting it to a cop? I should arrest you right now."

I peered at him anxiously. "Will you?"

He gave me an annoyed look. "No, but only because, as of right now, you're on the case with me as a consultant. But you had better get that book back before anyone realizes it's gone."

"Yes, sir," I said, over-seriously.

He shot me a dirty look, to which I grinned. He rolled his eyes at me, then turned serious once more. "Since you're part of the case, you should know more about it. Carter died from a blow to the head, which may or may not have been caused by the accident. The M.E. also found a strange fluid on Adam's fingers, but we had to send it off to be analyzed."

"M.E.?" I asked.

"Medical Examiner."

Right. I knew that. "How long until the analysis is returned?"

"We're not sure. The lab is backed up." Liam sighed. "This is what is most frustrating about working in a small town. We have a severe lack of resources."

"Okay... but until we find out what it is, what do we do?"

Liam sucked on his cheek, his handsome face growing more serious. "I'm not sure yet. But one thing is for sure. Sophie and Victor know more than what they're saying. The only question is, are they guilty of more than lying?"

# 4

# LOVE LETTERS AND SECRET MESSAGES

The next day, I tucked the copy of Shakespeare into my purse as I got ready to head back to Sophie's place. I had made discreet inquiries with Ella and learned that Victor worked at the bank, and so had stopped by as an excuse to see if he was working. He was, which meant I'd have time to deal with Sophie on my own.

If she was there, that is. I hoped she would be at work, too, but I had no excuse to check that out.

"Alright, here we go," I muttered as I smoothed out the two copies of Adam's letters to her.

The one from the Tragedies was even worse than the first one.

*To live, to love, to laugh, to weep, to hate*
*To die? What thoughts plague my scattered mind*
*Oh, but you are the end of my great weight*
*Do you see the light you bring? I am blind*

*Blinded by you, my heart, by you, my love*
*You! The angel. You! The dawn. You! My light*
*Ah, how I wish that I were but a dove*
*To follow you, my heart, all through the night*

*But I am a shadow within your life*
*And without that light, I wander to death*
*The road is long and filled with too much strife*
*I'm lost, my love, and no longer draw breath*

*I love you and all that you love as well*
*Your enemies: mine. Your hate: mine. Me? Yours.*

The pain seemed to scream off the page, and I suspected why that was. Spirits would often linger in the land of the living for too long if they'd left something unsaid. Adam might have remained tethered by these poems full of unrequited feelings.

And betrayal. The one from Sophie and Victor's house was dated only two weeks ago; so when Sophie said she hadn't spoken to Adam for three months, it wasn't entirely the full truth.

I let out a shuddering breath as I left the letters and headed out. I snagged a batch of cookies from Abigail the previous night, and I tucked the Tupperware container under my arm as I headed into the February chill. It was colder today than it had been the last few days, making me wonder if this was a sign.

Sophie was at her house when I rang the doorbell and was pleasantly surprised to receive the cookies. She looked surprised and suspicious when she first saw me, but when I offered the cookies, she relaxed and invited me in.

"I'm very sorry for intruding on you again," I told her as I set my purse on the floor behind the couch. I sat down as she sat across from me, next to the nightstand where I'd found the book of Shakespeare in the first place. "I just felt awful about bringing up so many terrible memories yesterday when I wanted to do the opposite."

"No, don't feel bad. It's not your fault. I'm just glad I could read that poem. It sounds awful, but I think he might have finally realized that there was nothing between us anymore." Sophie sighed as she nibbled a cookie.

"I'm sorry all the same," I said.

I cupped one hand, hiding it from her, and wriggled my fingers. My shifting wind tickled the tips of my fingers and flowed beneath the couch to flip open my purse. It struggled against the heavy tome; this was going to take a while.

Luckily, Sophie seemed very willing to talk. "After you and the detective left yesterday, I called Adam's family and had a hard conversation with them. Apparently, he never understood why I cut him off. They didn't even know we'd broken up. According to them, they thought we were still high school sweethearts going strong."

"That must be so rough," I said, inching the book along behind the couch.

Sophie closed the Tupperware. "It is. But I guess there's nothing I can really do now. Adam just acted so out of character. He seemed confused and paranoid. I was scared he was on drugs."

"Liam hasn't told me he was... but then," I lifted both my hands into a shrug. "He doesn't tell me about these things. He takes people's privacy very seriously."

I made a mental note to relay this information to Liam. If Adam's family still thought they were dating, then maybe Sophie was lying about breaking up with him, too? For that matter, we needed to make sure that she and Victor really were married! This whole situation was very complicated.

"I don't want to be rude..." Sophie winced.

I stood, using my winds to slide the Shakespeare book under the side table it'd been on yesterday. Sophie would think that it fell somehow; after all, she'd had her eyes on me this whole time and I was nowhere near the side table.

"I'm sorry for taking up your time," I told her. "I'll get out of your hair."

·· ◆ ··

Back at my store, I gathered a few artifacts I had scattered around my shop and took them into the back. Once there, I set up my things. A bell, a crystal, a candle, and, of course, the copies of the letters.

I set my hands palm-up on the table and focused. My flames jumped to life in my hands and I whispered to my winds, pulling the flames into a circle connecting the various artifacts.

"If the dead be here, let them speak," I said to the empty room.

One paper stirred slightly, but nothing happened. My flames went out. I thought this might happen; I grabbed a pencil and notepad and started scribbling down an incantation. Since Adam's words were written as sonnets, I needed to do the same.

It took me longer than I cared to admit, but finally, I was ready. I cleared my throat and called on my flames and wind.

Then I spoke.

> *"If the dead linger yet here, let them speak*
> *The love that was once bright and clear of mind*
> *The dead left a voice, so let that voice seek*
> *A path through the shadow, to this place find*
>
> *Adam Carter was taken young, too soon*
> *His words left unfinished, we now unlock*
> *Tell me the tale that once spun 'neath the moon*
> *Give me the words that he never did talk*
>
> *One last plea to the dead, one last refrain*
> *To hear the fresh words that never did come*
> *Hear me, I say, I know your heart remains*
> *Speak to me, Adam, and tell your death sum*
>
> *No more remain in the bleak, dark divide*
> *Tell me your truth so your pain may subside."*

The sound of a sigh filled the air. I held my breath, waiting as I glanced around, expecting to see Adam at any moment. But he never arrived. The two pages in the center of my circle lifted into the air and a voice, soft and sweet, began to speak.

"Your sunlight casts o'er the long road so bleak
Lifting both heart and soul of the weary one
A sadness now betrayed by one so meek
My life, my love, my heart, my joy, my sun."

As the voice read the poem, each word lit up. Every so often, one flared a brighter color. Looking closer, I realized what had been strange about the letters—some of them were written in thicker ink, others at a different slant.

I started scribbling down the words as they were read, catching the emphasis whenever it came up. When the letters were read, the flames went out and another sigh slipped through the air before disappearing.

My heart pounded as I looked at the two scribbled passages I'd been left with. These weren't just love letters. Adam Carter left behind secret messages... messages that pointed to his killer.

I yanked my phone from my pocket and snapped a picture of the two phrases and sent them to Liam. I'd uncovered a motive for murder.

I grabbed the letters and stuffed them into my pocket for proof as the bell rang, indicating someone had entered the bookshop. Ugh, hadn't I locked that? I must have forgotten.

I ran my fingers through my hair, making myself presentable, and stepped into the shop. Only to stop, eyes widening, when I saw who it was. Sophie stood in the bookshop, the Shakespeare's Tragedies in her arms. As soon as I stepped through the door, her gaze turned to me.

Oh, boy. That wasn't the look of someone who was bringing the book in to share that there was a letter in it. It wasn't the look of a person who had arrived to help resolve a mystery. It was someone who had suspicions of their own.

"Did you steal this from me?" she demanded.

I put on my best confused expression. "Steal what?"

"This?" She held the book in the air.

"I don't recall seeing it. Where was it? Maybe someone left it on the counter while I was out." Yeah, or she brought it in with her— because I'd left it in her house!

She slammed the book onto the counter, panting. "You know that's not what I mean. I mean it was in my house, then after you and your detective boyfriend showed up, it disappeared. Then you come back today and it's there again. I don't know how you did it, but you stole it from me!"

I lifted my hands into the air, attempting to look confused.

"Sophie, I don't know what you're talking about. Why don't we go over to Ella's Wheel and we can discuss this over a cup of coffee?"

Sophie turned toward the door. But instead of heading out, she locked the door and wheeled back around. Her hands clenched into fists, revealing just how muscular her arms were.

My heartbeat thrummed. Adam was one thing, but was she going to kill me, too?

I had to get out of there. I had to tell Liam.

"Sophie—" I started.

"There's only one reason you and the detective would take such a keen interest in my relationship with Adam," Sophie spat at me. "So, what happened? What do you know about Adam's death, Harper?"

I backed away from her as she stalked forward. "I don't know anything. That it was an accident. That—"

"Don't give me that!" Sophie breathed heavily as she glowered at me. "I want to know the truth. What do you know? Why did you steal my book?"

I opened my mouth and closed it again. Could I bolt for the door? With a rising anxiety, I saw a hunting knife sheathed at Sophie's waist. I couldn't run... not unless I wanted to be stabbed in the back.

## 5

# HEARTBREAK IN MOONHAVEN

"Nothing is happening," I said, inching toward the counter. If I could get behind it, I could press the panic button.

I couldn't use my magic without her seeing. And then I'd have a whole other problem on my hands. As much as I wanted to just knock her out with one of my winds, I couldn't reveal myself to Moonhaven. It didn't matter if most people wouldn't believe her. All it took was one witch hunter, and I was dead.

"Don't lie to me," Sophie hissed.

"Look, whatever you think—"

I cut myself off, yelping, when she pulled the hunting knife. She waved it in my face, her eyes wide and furious. Her hands shook. How much provocation could she stand before she struck? My throat went dry.

Of course, getting stabbed would kill me much more efficiently than a witch hunter. So maybe magic was the only way out of this.

"You stole my book. You found the letter," Sophie said, her shaking hand clenched tighter over the knife. "Why? Why did you have to invade my privacy like that? What purpose could you possibly have?"

"Sophie, put down the knife. It will not help anyone."

Sophie shook her hair, her jaw clenching. "Get into the back."

Oh, no. If I did that, nobody on the street could see what was happening and call for help. On the other hand, it would also allow me to use my magic with no witnesses. I took a deep breath, trying to calm myself enough to think clearly.

Yes. Get into the back and use magic to disarm her if necessary. I just needed to keep enough distance between the two of us so she couldn't easily stab me.

I walked backward, watching to make sure she wasn't going to suddenly lunge. As soon as we were back there, I scooted around the table so it was between us. Sophie glanced around, her eyebrows knitting when she saw the setup from my ritual. She slammed the door behind us.

"Now, you're going to answer me," she said.

I pulled the two copies of the letters from my pocket. "I needed to check them both."

Sophie's face twisted with anger. She held out her empty hand. "Give me those! They're meant to be private. Adam wrote them for me!"

I laid the papers on the table.

She was going to figure out that I'd learned the secret message. I took a deep breath.

"You won't gain anything by killing me, Sophie. I have cameras in the front, they upload to the cloud. Only Liam and I have access to it. He'll know what happened. So put down the knife. He's already on his way here. You don't want to make this worse for yourself than it already is.'"

Sophie shook her head hard. "I never said I was going to kill you."

"You're threatening me with a knife! You don't need to say anything," I pointed out. I lowered my hands to hide them beneath the table and moved my fingers in the way to summon a wind. Not yet, though—I might get through to her. "As for Adam, we already know. I already sent the evidence to Liam."

"Evidence?"

I paused. She looked truly startled... but wasn't that why she was here? To find out how much I'd figured out already?

"We found the messages Adam left in those letters. We know what you did. The only thing is, why? You said he was acting erratically. Had he threatened you?" I asked, trying to make my voice lower and soothing.

Maybe I could convince her I was on her side.

"Secret message?" Sophie looked bewildered. "What secret message?"

The knife lowered a bit, and she stared at the papers, completely distracted. If I wasn't so startled by her reaction, I might have had the wherewithal to leap across the table to wrestle the knife away from her. But I was too stunned to move a muscle.

Either she was the best actress in the world, or she had no idea what I was talking about.

"He put messages in his letters," I told her. I turned to one paper and pointed out what was written just a little differently from the other ones. "He knew what you were doing?"

"Of course he did! I told him all about Victor."

I frowned. Her confusion was even more palpable. Despite everything I'd concluded up to this point, as I stared at her, I realized she wasn't the killer after all... so who was?

"Sophie."

She looked up at me, looking lost and not at all threatening.

"Put the knife down. It will help no one," I whispered.

She inhaled sharply, released a tremulous breath, then dropped the knife. She crumpled into a chair and hid her face in both hands. Her shoulders shook as sobs ripped through her. She curled inward, as though she was trying to stop herself from literally falling to pieces.

A crashing noise from the front of the bookstore made me jump. I hurried to the front to find Liam rushing in, frigid winter air swirling around him through the broken glass of the front door.

Relief washed over his face when he saw me unharmed. He grabbed my wrist and spun me behind him before I could even greet him. He had his Taser out and ready.

"Ella called in that Sophie was here," he whispered.

"She's in the back. I'm okay. She didn't hurt me."

Liam's gaze searched me for any sign that I was lying, then nodded.

His face tightened. "Sophie, I know you're back there. Come out with your hands in the air."

He held the Taser in both hands. Sophie stepped around the doorframe, her hands in the air over her head. Tears ran down her cheeks. She didn't look afraid, only resigned. Liam took the handcuffs off his belt and I grabbed his wrist.

"That's not necessary. She's not going to fight. She didn't kill Adam."

Sophie's hands lowered slightly. "You think I killed Adam?"

Liam hesitated. "Harper, she's still dangerous."

I shook my head. "Trust me on this one. She will not hurt anyone."

Liam studied me, then Sophie. He must have seen something in both of us he believed because he put both the handcuffs and Taser away. Sophie wrapped her arms around her middle.

"You still have to arrest me. I threatened Harper with a knife. So you have to arrest me," she said.

"He can arrest you in a bit," I said, stepping past him. I held out the paper that I'd scrawled the secret messages on. "This is what Adam wrote."

*To what end do you wish for my death? I love you. You hate me.*

*Your heart betrayed my love. My death is at your hand. Let me go.*

Sophie took it carefully, fresh tears spilling. "I had to cut off Adam because he was acting so strangely. Sometimes, it was like he forgot who I was. Other times, it was like he thought we were still dating. I told him all about Victor, but more than once when he came to my house to find Victor, he'd go into a rage, accusing me of cheating on him. I had to cut him off."

"And these messages, they seem to say that he thought you were trying to kill him," I pointed out. "At least, that's how I read them first. But maybe it was just a metaphor. He said that you were killing him because of your rejection."

Sophie shook her head, her eyes wide. "I never would have hurt him. I begged him to get help. I thought he was on drugs or something was wrong. He refused to tell me anything. I just couldn't keep going."

Liam's voice was hard. "He had no alcohol in his system the night he died. His brakes, however, were cut."

"And you think I...?" Sophie covered her mouth with her hand, her face paling.

"I did, but I don't anymore," I admitted. "You're an automobile mechanic. His brakes were cut. There was clearly a love triangle happening with you, Adam, and Victor."

Liam crossed his arms. "And if you felt threatened by him, it gives you even more reason to do away with him."

Sophie flinched. "I didn't kill him! But..." She bowed her head and her breath hitched. "But I think I know who maybe did."

My stomach twisted. Now that she said it... I had a terrible feeling that maybe I knew, too.

"Tell us everything," Liam ordered.

"I really did love him. I wish I could have done more for him..." Sophie shook her head and sobbed once more. She sank to the floor, as though she didn't have the strength to hold herself up. "I wish... I wish things were different. I wish..."

I knelt beside her, despite Liam's warning glance. I put an arm around her shoulders, trying to comfort her.

"Start at the beginning," I urged her. "When you first started noticing something was off about him."

# 6

## CUPID'S FINAL ARROW

"Thank you, Harper," Liam said as I handed him a mug of elderberry tea.

"I hope you enjoy it. It's my own recipe," I said as I sat next to him. He and I were in the living room of Abigail's B&B.

Abigail and Ella were sitting across from us. Abigail had a tea of her own, while Ella was sipping on a decaf coffee she'd brought in from work. She twitched with anticipation, her eyes continually darting from Liam and me.

With Sophie having been officially cleared and the Adam Carter case closed, Liam and I were finally at liberty to tell what happened. To think it all started with a sonnet on Valentine's Day... I shook my head, sighing as my heart twisted.

"Don't keep me in suspense," Ella begged, leaning forward. "There are all sorts of rumors flying around town. People are saying that Victor murdered Adam for Sophie's love, or that Adam threatened to kill Sophie and so Victor killed him to protect her."

My hands tightened on the mug. Of course, tawdry rumors were flying! But then... hadn't I made assumptions of my own during this case? It would be a really poor showing on my part to condemn other people for the same thoughts that had run through my head.

"That rumor isn't anywhere near the truth," I said. "It's a vicious lie and needs to be killed."

Ella's expression faltered. "I haven't been sharing it."

I winced. "Sorry. I didn't mean to accuse you. It's just that the situation is so tragic already... I didn't mean to snap."

"It's okay." Ella smiled at me.

Abigail sighed. "So, what did happen? If it wasn't an accident and it wasn't murder, what does it leave?"

"Suicide," Liam answered.

His proclamation sat heavy in the air. Ella's eyes widened and Abigail bowed her head, as though she had been expecting that answer, but hoped that it wasn't the case.

I set my tea aside. Even now, it made my chest tighten to think about how all the pieces fell into place. Sophie's tale about Adam's behavior caused Liam to go back to the autopsy report. To the prescription medications in his system. The ones that led us to his medical reports and answered all the questions.

"That's awful," Ella murmured. "When it was all rumor and suspects, I could almost forget how horrible the situation actually was."

She hung her head, ashamed of herself.

"It's a coping mechanism." Abigail sipped her tea. "You can't beat yourself up for wanting to put distance between yourself and the pain. Everyone loves a story that allows them to feel something other than sorrow or indifference."

Ella chewed her lip.

"The thing is, we're not even sure if it was on purpose," I said slowly. I glanced at Liam. "The case documents are public record now, right?"

"Yes. The judge ruled for it to be open," he said.

I turned back to Ella. "Adam was diagnosed two years ago with early onset dementia. It's not something anyone would have suspected at his age. But he didn't tell anyone, not even his own family. I guess he thought he could manage it on his own."

Liam reached over to take my hand in his. "He was overdosing on his medications. That, combined with the symptoms of dementia, caused him to behave erratically."

"Shouldn't he have had someone to help him?" Ella asked, stricken.

"Who? He didn't tell anyone. He was lying to his doctors about his symptoms and support system. He lived alone." Liam shook his head. "He wasn't a social person even before the disease. He didn't have people close enough to see what was really happening."

"His last lifeline was Sophie, but his possessive behavior grew increasingly dangerous to her," I said, shaking my head.

I couldn't imagine what it must have been like to witness such a dramatic change in his behavior and not know why. Sophie had shared how deeply it frightened her and the trauma she had left from Adam's actions was still obvious. She blamed herself, even though there wasn't anything she could have done.

From the outside, he became jealous, paranoid, and angry. It was explained by his disease, but who would expect that an otherwise healthy twenty-something young man would develop something like dementia?

"When she broke communication with him, he blamed it on her getting together with Victor," Liam picked up. "Even though she had been dating Victor for some time, in his mind, he and Sophie were still dating. He was convinced that she was cheating on him and grew more and more paranoid."

"The letter," Ella said. "That's why he was talking about betrayal and darkness and light. Because he was still in love with her, but thought she betrayed him."

I nodded. "I think in his more lucid moments, he tried to reach out for help in those letters. But he never told her directly. There wasn't anything she could have done."

Abigail sighed as she rubbed her neck. "You said there were secret messages in the letters. Those weren't about his illness. So where did they come from?

"Adam became convinced that Sophie was trying to kill him, to clear her way to be with Victor. He left messages behind in his love letters, accusing her of wanting him dead. He wasn't seeing the situation straight." I rubbed my tired eyes.

That was also the reason I only heard his voice and never his spirit when I performed his ritual. His spirit hadn't lingered on this plane. Once he died, he had moved on. The only thing left behind was the voice he recorded in his written word.

"He should have been in a care facility," Abigail said.

"He should have. That's what makes it so tragic," Liam agreed.

Ella sighed. "What about the book of Shakespeare's Sonnets? Did he throw it out, or did Sophie?"

"They were Adam's books. He was leaving them on her doorstep. Victor admitted that when he came home one day to find another one, he took it upon himself to get rid of it," Liam explained. "He was tired of the confusion, fear, and turmoil it put Sophie through."

"Understandable," Abigail said.

Ella frowned. "It wasn't his possession to throw out."

"Regardless, he thought he was protecting the woman he loved," I pointed out.

Liam shifted in his seat. "The better thing to do would have been to bring it to the station and let us deal with it. I understand why he didn't, though. He didn't want things to escalate until someone got hurt. Not even Adam."

I sighed and continued the story. "When Sophie and Victor eloped, Adam saw them in the bar together. He must have seen their rings and drank one beer. There were the barest traces of alcohol in his system, so little that the M.E. missed it entirely."

"But he was on medication," Ella whispered, understanding in her eyes. "Let me guess... medication that doesn't mix well with alcohol."

"Enough so that we'll never know why he cut his own brake lines," Liam said. He looked tired; it had been a strange and difficult case. I reached for his hand and squeezed it lightly. He squeezed back, smiling at me. "Sophie taught him how to maintain his vehicle and we found brake fluid on his hands."

I nodded. "In his state, though, he could have convinced himself that Sophie had done something to the brakes, and he was fixing them. Or he could have been setting her up. Or he might have just wanted to die. We'll never know."

"And so that's what caused the crash," Ella murmured. "That's... far more tragic than any of the rumors spreading. I'll ask to put a notice in the newspaper explaining the actual story so that people stop accusing Victor and Sophie."

I nodded at her, relieved. They had already suffered enough. The last thing they deserved was for people to be throwing accusations at them behind their backs.

"If he'd just shared his diagnosis, Sophie and his family could have helped him," Abigail murmured. "And not just them. I'd have helped him, too. Goodness knows I've had friends go through the same thing."

Ella wrapped her arms around her waist. "I would have tried to help, too. I wish I'd noticed something. He came in so regularly. To think that he was going through so much and nobody knew."

Liam shook his head as he leaned his elbows on his knees. "His doctors failed him. They should have been more proactive."

"Maybe if they had better resources and funding, they would have been able to help him. He didn't have a regular physician, he only ever went to walk-in clinics," I reminded Liam gently. "I don't think playing the blame game helps. I think it's just tragic."

"Tragedy always follows when Cupid's arrow hits the wrong mark," Abigail said. She got to her feet. "I don't know about all of you, but I need something sweet to help counter this bitter discussion. Ella, come help me get some cookies."

"Sure."

They exited for the kitchen, leaving Liam and me alone. We were quiet for a long moment, each of us lost in our own thoughts, before Liam turned to me. He took my hand once more, pressing both of his over it. His clear blue eyes gazed straight into mine.

Goosebumps rose on my arms. Liam had never looked so intently at me before. My heart skipped a beat as I gazed back at him.

"What is it?" I asked nervously.

"I wanted to thank you. I'm not sure I would have been able to solve the case if you weren't involved in it. I was so focused on the facts and what I saw right there, I didn't consider other possibilities." He took a deep breath and let out it, looking pained to admit it. "Your intuition saved Sophie from some ugly accusations."

"I assumed she was guilty at first, too."

Liam shook his head. "Only because of the evidence I gathered, and how I presented it to you."

"I wouldn't go that far." I squeezed both of his hands. "I'm only sad that this whole thing happened at all."

We were quiet again. Rather than being lost in our own thoughts, though, it was being comfortable in each other's presence. The sounds of Abigail and Ella clattering around in the kitchen seemed distant as we sat there.

Eventually, Liam smiled. "Next time, I hope it's not a death that pushes us to spend more time together."

I blushed as I grinned. "Me, too."

<br>

The End

Did you enjoy *Valentine Vendetta*?

Please consider rating it on Amazon, Goodreads, or Bookbub.

Reviews help me reach new readers.

Read **Equinox Enigma**, the next story in the **Mystic Moonhaven Mysteries.**

<br>

Have you read the *Jane and Kennedy Daniels Mysteries*, the *Annie Archer Paranormal Mysteries*, the *Wilma Wade Holiday Mysteries,* the *Mike and Maddie Mysteries,* or the *Pine Grove Mysteries?*

# 1

# EQUINOX AWAKENING

My breath puffed out in a cloud of fog, making me wrinkle my nose. I had hoped this strange cold front would lift once we got out of February, but it was hanging on. It shouldn't be this cold this time of year.

"You okay, Harper?" my walking companion asked.

Detective Liam Ashford and I had gotten into the habit of taking early morning walks before he had to go to the police station and I had to open my bookshop. Normally, we had quite a lively conversation about everything from a TV show we were both watching to whatever newest gossip my friend Ella had to share about our small town, Moonhaven.

"I'm sorry I've been quiet today," I apologized to Liam. "It's the weather. I'm so tired of winter. I know I've only been in Moonhaven for a little over a year, but I don't remember March last year being so cold and snowy still."

"That's because it's usually not," Liam answered. "Moonhaven is usually very mild, especially for this part of the country."

I hummed, shoving my hands into my pockets as a chilly breeze ruffled my hair. "It's going to be the spring equinox in a few days."

Liam snorted and gave me an amused look. "You're not going to say that the equinox has some sort of mystical effect on whether it snows, are you?"

I rolled my eyes at him. The spring equinox was a powerful time for magic, not that Liam would believe it. His feet were firmly planted on the ground, to the point of coming up with perfectly rational explanations for the irrational things that happened around Moonhaven. He had a hard enough time not commenting on the various occult books and crystals I sell at my bookstore.

Sometimes I wondered what his reaction would be if I told him I was a witch. Not that I would—secrecy was the number one rule in these things. So even though I was certain I could summon my flames or winds right in front of him and he still wouldn't believe me, I would not risk it.

"If you think about it, the equinox has the power to stop it from snowing. Seeing as how spring ends the winter," I teased him.

There seemed to be something off this year, though. It had started way back at the beginning of the year when Percival Whitman used ancestral magic to attack the town. The underlying magical disturbance that it caused had lingered ever since and was getting stronger the closer we got to the equinox.

"Ha ha," Liam said, bumping me with his shoulder. "Hilarious."

I stuck my tongue out at him. By this time, we had reached the Bed & Breakfast where I'd ended up as my temporary permanent residence.

Moonhaven didn't have much of a real estate market, and finding an affordable place to live so far had been impossible. I owned my little bookstore outright, though, and was currently trying to figure out if I could build a second floor so I could live where I worked.

The owner of the B&B, Abigail Thorne, was in the living room, shaking her head as she flipped through a book of folk remedies when Liam and I came in.

"Don't bother thinking about a shower," she said, sounding frazzled. "The town just put out a notice. The pipes have frozen up, so there's no running water. They're seeing if they can ship in some bottled water from other towns while they try to fix the problem."

I unwound the scarf from my neck, frowning. "How could they freeze? They're under the ground."

"Don't ask me how." Abigail sighed. "I'm trying to find something that will help poor Ella. That cold of hers is just not going away."

"She should see a doctor," Liam said. He didn't take off his winter gear. "No water, huh? That makes it even worse. I hope we don't make the news. This kind of thing attracts weirdos and do-gooders, and I'm too cold to deal with the logistics."

He looked so disgruntled that I laughed. He hadn't worn a knitted hat today, so his dark hair was ruffled by the wind. With his flannel coat and barely there five o'clock shadow, he looked more like a lumberjack than a police detective. Once he shaved and put on his uniform, though, all ruggedness would disappear.

I had to admit, even though I was more of a firefighter or Coast Guard gal, something about Liam Ashford in his uniform made me confront an unfortunate truth: the man was the most attractive person in all of Moonhaven. And I liked to look at him almost as much as I enjoyed our banter.

"Sounds like you have something else going on," Abigail noted, closing the book of remedies for now. She kept her finger between the pages to mark her spot.

Liam shrugged, then sighed. "I might as well tell you. It'll be all over town soon enough. Someone keeps breaking into the museum. They've taken a few little, inconsequential things, but I can't figure out how or who it is."

"Didn't David Blackwood install security cameras?" I asked, frowning. David was the museum curator.

"That's the frustrating thing. He did. The tapes are all missing, though, and when we checked the cloud, there's nothing. The cover-up seems far too high-tech for what they're taking," Liam explained. "Max Harrington is taking an unnatural interest in it all and, if I had a suspect, it'd be him."

I considered his words. I knew little about Max Harrington, other than he was an old friend of Ella's. But Ella had so many friends in Moonhaven, that didn't give me much to go on.

"Why do you say 'if' you had a suspect, if you suspect Max?"

Abigail asked. Her crinkled eyes were cunning as she picked up on what I'd missed.

Liam grimaced. "I have no proof connecting him. No motive. Nothing. They might as well be disappearing into the ether for what I've been able to find out."

A shiver ran down my spine. "Could it be connected to the Winter Festival?" Percival Whitman tried to steal the documents that proved his family stole the Blackwood land when the town was first founded.

"No. What use would he have for a handkerchief and a teacup? Whitman is in jail for his crimes and there's no reason for him to be attacking the museum."

"Unless he wanted to set up David for something in vengeance," I pointed out.

Then there was what Liam didn't know. Percival had called on an ancient magic in his attacks. A magic that had a lingering disturbance in town. The land issue was still being disputed by both the Blackwoods and the Whitmans. For now, it was in a town trust. The museum had been at the heart of the previous attacks.

It could be at the heart of this disturbance as well.

"Hey." Liam gently took my hand and squeezed. "My guess is that this is all going to blow over. Someone thinks they're being funny. I'm sure nothing will come of it."

I forced a smile in return, not at all confident.

Liam gave my hand one last reassuring squeeze and then turned to go. "I'll call you later."

"Come over for dinner," Abigail offered. "I'm making Shepherd's Pie."

"I'll see if I can make it," Liam promised. He touched his forehead as though tipping his hat. "Ladies."

He opened the door. A burst of fresh cold brought with it the bite of frost. I shivered, my arms wrapped around myself. How did it get colder outside in the few minutes that we were in here?

Abigail hummed as she tapped her chin. "Every thief has a story. Seek the heart, and you'll find more than stolen relics."

Heat blossomed in my cheeks. "Wh-what?"

"Nothing, dear. Come with me. I have something to show you in the greenhouse." Abigail smiled brightly, knowingly, and led me through the B&B.

My face remained hot as I followed. Was Abigail talking about my relationship with Liam? Yes, we'd grown closer over these last few months... At least, I no longer held his pragmatism against him, and he tolerated my wild flights of fancy. Was Abigail telling me to join the case so I could spend more time with him?

Come to think about it, that might not be such a bad idea.

Abigail's greenhouse was connected to the house, and an addition of glass was built onto the south side. Thanks to the space heaters she'd put out here, it was warm and toasty. The sun beamed through the windows, making it feel like spring ought to. The rows on rows of planters we had worked on over the last few months were burgeoning with life.

"Oh, it's beautiful," I exclaimed, clapping my hands lightly.

"Isn't it?" Abigail checked the soil of her row of daffodils. "Even the winter can't hold out forever. New life is blossoming, even if we can't see it everywhere. Feel free to come out here whenever you need to, Harper. I know the constant snow and cold weighs on one's soul."

"Thank you."

I settled into a wicker chair, enjoying the scent of warm soil and plants. As I sat there, surrounded by the growing plants, I felt lighter than I had during my walk with Liam. I hadn't even realized how much of a weight the snow was having on me.

Sitting here, it became all the clearer that something wrong was happening. Whether Percival was behind bars, I knew this was connected to the strange things happening in the museum. Which meant I needed to investigate.

Liam was a brilliant detective, but he was in over his head if magic was involved.

I pulled out my phone and sent him a text.

> I want in on this case with you.

It took a few minutes for him to reply.

> There's barely a case. I can handle it.

> Never said you couldn't. But we said we wanted to work on a case together that hadn't escalated to death or disappearances, right?

I held my breath, waiting. When he didn't answer, I sent another text.

> This would be perfect since you said it was probably nothing big. We could make it an official work-together case.

> Come to the police station at ten. I'll get the paperwork done to make you an official consultant.

I sent a thumbs up and slid my phone back into my pocket, grinning. There. That was the first step in figuring out what was going on. Now for the hard part.

## 2

## LOST LEGACY

Ella's Wheel was the most popular coffee shop in Moonhaven. Ella ran the place, and everyone was always eager to see her bright disposition when they showed up. It had been closed for the past week because of Ella's head cold. When I contacted David Blackwood to talk with him about the museum case, he insisted that our meeting happen at the shop.

Ella had, apparently, already agreed. She lived over the shop, so it was easy enough for her to run down and open it up.

"Are you sure?" I asked her as I made coffee with the shiny machine behind the brew bar.

She sat in a booth, nose red and honey-brown hair piled on her head. But she smiled at me. "Oh, I'm more than sure. I've been so bored! I don't even feel that sick. I just don't want to spread my germs all over town."

The door opened, and David Blackwood stepped in. He was a man of medium height and had an academic air. He smiled politely, but he seemed nervous when he looked at me.

"David, take a seat," I told him. "Ella said you asked her to be here, too?"

"If it's alright," he said, sliding into the booth opposite her as she hastily put on a cloth mask and used hand sanitizer on her hands. She took the whole not spreading germs thing seriously.

"It's fine," I assured him. "I am here as an official consultant with the police, but I asked Liam, and he said it was fine. I'll have to record our conversation, though."

David nodded stiffly.

"You want anything?" I asked as I set my finished coffee on the brew bar.

"Decaf, one milk, and sugar," Ella said behind her mask.

David visibly relaxed as he nodded.

As I brewed up the cup for him, a knock came on the door. I turned, and my eyes widened. Max Harrington, Liam's closest thing to a suspect, stood on the other side of the door. Ella scooted out of the booth and answered it.

"I picked you up some cough drops," Max told her. He glanced at David and me but didn't comment. "I hope you feel better."

"Thanks," Ella told me.

Max smiled. "If you need anything—"

"I know. I could use some of your famous Italian wedding soup later."

"I'll bring some around," he promised.

He left, and Ella popped one of the cough drops into her mouth before she sanitized her hands again and returned to the booth. By then, I'd finished the coffee and brought it over. I gave David his decaf and sat next to Ella. I put my phone on record and put it on the table between us.

"This is Harper Nightshade talking with Ella Grace and David Blackwood," I said. "Detective Liam Ashford asked me to talk to you, David, to see if I could offer any insights into what's happening at the museum. Would you like to tell me about the artifacts that were stolen?"

David fidgeted as he stared at the cup in his hands. "A handkerchief that belonged to William Blackwood. A teacup belonging to Charles Whitman. A kettle that belonged to Herbert Sinclair. A plow that belonged to Laurence Mercer, and a sad iron that belonged to the Harrington family."

"A sad iron?" Ella asked.

David turned to her. "Those old irons made from solid iron, heated on the fire, and then used to press clothes. They're called sad irons."

I tapped my chin, thinking. "Those were the five families that founded Moonhaven, weren't they?"

David nodded. "Outside of the town, they have very little worth, though. I can't imagine why anyone would steal them. It's not like you could get anything on the black market for any of it."

On the other hand, it was potentially worth a lot in magic if this was connected to the ancestral magic that Percival used back in January. I'd need to know more about these five founding families.

Abigail had said to seek the heart. Now, she might have been talking about Liam, but she always seemed to know more about what was happening in Moonhaven than she let on. Plus, she'd lived here her whole life, and if anyone would know the town's secret history, it was her.

"This might sound strange, but were there any love affairs between the families?" I asked David. "We know that the Blackwood lands were stolen because Howard Whitman claimed he was married to Penelope Blackwood when he wasn't. Someone might try to use these artifacts to prove something."

"Like what?" Ella asked.

I laughed self-consciously and shrugged. "I'm not sure. But it's worth thinking about, right?"

David looked less than certain, but Ella swallowed my lie. Her eyes sparkled as she leaned forward across the table. "It's a great story, anyway. So. Any sordid love affairs?"

"I'm not sure sordid is the right word," David replied. "But while I was reading her journals, I realized that Penelope Blackwood was in love with Herbert Sinclair. There are no records anything came from it, though."

I leaned back, disappointed. "What about the other families?"

"There were marriages for sure. But nothing particularly scandalous."

Ella hummed as she popped another cough drop into her mouth. "You know what? I've been looking into my family history, and my mother was a descendant of Herbert Sinclair and my father was a descendant of Charles Whitman. If you think about it, Moonhaven's history is four hundred years old. I bet there were a lot of intermarriages between the families since then."

That was a fair point. Just because someone didn't have the same last name as the founding families didn't mean they couldn't have inherited their magic books.

I sighed, resting my chin in my hand. This really didn't get me anywhere closer to where I needed to be. "I doubt that it's someone who thinks that because they're descended from the founders, it means they should have their belongings."

Ella frowned. "You wouldn't think so, but maybe there is. People can be weird sometimes. When I researched my family tree, I went to the cemetery to double-check the dates on the documents I'd found and Percival Whitman just about blew his top when he saw me in the Whitman family section."

David winced at the mention of the man who had attacked him.

"But then we all know that he's not exactly stable," Ella said quickly. She blushed.

"It's fine," David told her. "I don't mind."

I, however, was piqued by this turn of events. "You were researching your family history even before the Winter Festival? You've never brought it up before."

Ella shrugged. "I guess I never thought about it with you. We have so many other things we're talking about. I've been working with Max a lot. Hey, actually, did you know David and I are distant cousins? It's all very amusing."

I smiled at her, but I had a funny feeling sink into my stomach. It seemed strange that she would work with Max Harrington to look into her family tree and not bring anything up.

She sneezed, covering her masked face with both hands, then grabbed the sanitizer.

"Why don't you go wash your hands instead of using more of that stuff?" I suggested, moving out of the booth. "Your skin will dry up, and your hands will crack."

"I really should get back to the museum anyway," David said.

"Do you mind if I come along with you? I'd like to look around," I blurted. Ella was looking tired, her cheeks pink with a fever.

I almost took back my question so I could take Ella to the hospital, but she caught my eye and frowned. "Don't go worrying over me, Harper. That's what everyone's doing. Abigail's going to be over here before you know it. I'm fine. You go on with David."

David hadn't actually agreed to take me to the museum. The disgruntled expression on his face told me he would rather I didn't go. But Ella was looking so miserable he apparently didn't want to say no in front of her.

We took our coffee to-go, and I made Ella promise to text me if she got worse. Then David and I headed toward the museum in his car. I'd call Liam to come pick me up so I could fill him in with what little I'd found out.

The drive was tense, but as we drew closer to the museum, David broke the silence.

"When I was in a coma in January, I kept seeing your face in my dreams," he said.

I bit my lips together. It wasn't surprising. His spirit kept coming to me while he was in his coma, giving me clues to find him.

"I'm sorry that I'm so on edge around you," he continued, his voice softening. "I don't mean to, but I still associate you with everything that happened."

"That's not your fault. I'm sorry that I'm making it worse for you."

David sighed. "But you saved me. I remember that much."

Something about the way he said it made goosebumps break out over my skin. Did he remember the magic that had taken him out into the woods in the first place? The frost wolfs that had dragged him away and nearly killed him?

I swallowed as I looked out the window. "I did what I could. It was all so frightening I barely remember anything."

"I've always wondered who the anonymous person who told Detective Ashford where to find me was," he prodded.

"Me, too," I said. I didn't have to act with that one. It was a complete mystery to me as well.

We arrived at the museum, only to find the front door wide open.

David groaned. "Great. It's happened again."

I took off my seatbelt nervously. "They won't be in there waiting for us, will they?"

"No. They're always gone. Besides, there's a back door. We just have to make a lot of noise," David assured me.

If he was calm about it, I saw no reason to be alarmed myself. I called Liam, and we headed inside.

"If you're still here, you'd better scram," David yelled. "We already called the police. I—"

He paused just inside the doorstop.

I ran into him and bounced off. "Sorry—"

Then I saw why he'd stopped. The glass case that stood in the middle of the welcome room was empty. My eyes widened as I scrambled to remember what was there... the bell. The big bronze bell that had to weigh half a ton was missing.

"How?" David breathed. "That bell has been part of Moonhaven since its founding. Why would anyone take it?"

## 3

# BLOOMING SECRETS

Liam arrived at the museum shortly. His anxious expression melted into relief once he saw both David and me sitting in the welcoming area. He strode over to us, only to falter when he noticed the empty display case.

"What happened?" he asked, his eyes widening.

"Someone stole the bell," David replied glumly.

I rubbed my arms as Liam ran a hand through his hair. "None of the alarms were tripped. What about the footage?"

David shook his head. "Same as before. Nothing. I guess we know what the thief was doing. They must have been testing the systems to see if they could pull it off. I don't get it."

"Is it valuable?" I asked. Until now, he'd been so lost in his own thoughts, I didn't want to ask.

"It's not worth much. Not in terms of pure materials or even for collectors. Bells like that aren't all that rare." David stood and paced to the display case. "It's not even the most valuable artifact in the museum."

Liam pulled out a little notebook and jotted down a few notes. "Was anything else taken this time?"

David shook his head. "Not that I've seen. I haven't taken a thorough look at the archives yet, though."

"Once you've completed that, get back to me," Liam said. His brow furrowed. "It seems this is bigger than we previously thought."

I stood. "David, do you have any books about the founding families? Everything that the thief has taken has been connected to something related to the founding of Moonhaven. Maybe there's something in history that will give us a motive."

David and Liam both looked skeptical, but when I met Liam's gaze, he nodded. I gave him a small smile in return. He might not understand everything I was doing, but he would let me take this in the direction I thought might lead somewhere. I was grateful for that.

"These books here are related to the founders," David said, pointing at a shelf of red-bound books. "The sign-out sheet is on my desk. I'll get it."

As he went to the desk, Liam shifted closer to me. "Want to share your hunch?"

"I think this might be another Percival situation. I just want to know if there's a reason for any of the families still in town to take any of these things. Trying to stake their claim or something," I whispered back.

Liam frowned at me. He searched my face, and I stared back, wondering what he was looking for.

Did he suspect that there was more than what I was letting on? He broke away before I could figure it out. I was left distinctly unsettled as David handed me the sign-out sheet. I wrote my name on them, then paused. Max Harrington had signed out each of the books several times since January. Coincidence?

He had seen David at the coffee shop earlier. He'd know that it was empty.

Once I had the books, Liam drove me back to the B&B. I told him about Max signing out the books and he nodded once, but said nothing in response.

Back at the B&B, I called up Ella. "Hey, you want to come to the inn and help me read through a bunch of dry history books?"

Ella laughed, sounding wheezy. "Yes, please. I'm bored out of my head."

I took the most promising book to the front room, where I sat reading and watching for Ella. She arrived shortly, dropped off by Max Harrington. I frowned. First, he showed up at the coffee shop and now this... did he suspect I was onto him?

Onto him how, though? I had only the vaguest suspicions about him and wouldn't even suspect him if Liam didn't.

"Oh, good," Abigail said when Ella came in. "I was just going to make myself a bit of tea. I'll whip something up to help you with that cold of yours."

Ella's eyes pinched into a smile, though her mouth was hidden by a mask. "That sounds wonderful. Thank you."

"I figure we can go out to the greenhouse to read there," I told her, clutching the book to my chest. "It'll be more pleasant in the fresh life of all those growing plants."

Ella glanced outside, where a fresh skiff of snow had dusted everything, and nodded fervently. We got set up, Abigail joining us. We each had a book and read in silence as we sipped at our tea. Mine felt warm and cozy, making me invigorated. I'd have to ask for the recipe—this was much better for concentration than coffee was.

"There were an awful lot of feuds between the five founding families," Ella said after some time. She had stopped coughing and looked much more relaxed and healthier. "It looks like the Sinclairs and the Blackwoods had a genuine friendship between the two. The Sinclairs helped the Blackwoods after they lost their lands to the Whitmans."

"And the Harringtons were linked with the Whitmans through marriage," I said, tracing my finger over the wedding registries I'd come across. "It seems like the Harringtons were always closely allied to them. It was the Harringtons that claimed to be witnesses to Howard Whitman marrying Penelope Blackwood."

Abigail sighed as she closed her book. "And there are so many accusations of theft and land disputes. It's a miracle that Moonhaven didn't tear itself apart."

She looked distinctly unsettled, but before I could ask for more about it, Ella shut her book with a snap. "I guess I should have read through these books while looking for my family history. As it turns out, I'm a direct descendant of all five of the original founders."

"Are you?" Abigail asked. Her brow furrowed.

"Looks like it. I—" Ella sneezed.

The hair on the back of my neck rose as a magical sensation swooshed through the air. The lights blinked off, and the space heater ground to a stop. My eyes widened even as the lingering heat of the greenhouse battled against the cold seeping through the glass windows.

Oh, no. Ella looked up at the lights with a bewildered expression. But I was putting together the dates. Moonhaven was getting warmer again... until Ella got sick. I'd originally thought she got sick because of the cold, but what if it was the other way around? Every time her fever spiked, we got a new snowfall.

Now she sneezed, and the power went out. Coincidence? Not with that magic I felt in the air with her.

"I'll go start a fire in the old wood stove," Abigail said, standing.

"Thanks," Ella croaked. She looked suddenly miserable, though moments ago she'd been healthy enough. She sipped her tea and spat it back out. "It's gone cold."

I stood and set my book aside. "Let's get inside. Don't want you getting colder than you already are."

Ella nodded, pulling her mask on again. She seemed weak now, so I helped her into the living room where Abigail worked on starting a fire. I bundled Ella into blankets, and while Abigail's back was turned to me, I whispered a spell and sent my seeking winds out around Ella.

"Ooh, there's a draft," she said, shivering.

The winds returned to me, relaying back what they had sensed. It made my stomach drop. Ella was in the crosshairs of a powerful, very complex spell. I couldn't get a closer read on it, but I knew it was bad.

Someone was stealing items that belonged to the founders of Moonhaven, and Ella was caught in a powerful spell that was freezing the town. That couldn't be a coincidence, either, which meant it was connected.

Connected to the events with Percival Whitman during the Winter Festival, too. History had shown the Harringtons were the Whitmans' stooges and Max Harrington was showing a peculiar interest in Ella. But why? What was he hoping to do? What was he going to get out of it all?

And, more importantly, was he a witch? Percival had an ancestral magic that he used to summon those frost-wolves. Is Max also using magic, or is this spell on Ella a latent spell in Moonhaven that was triggered by Percival's actions? With the amount of feuds in the founding families, they could have cursed each other.

Ella was descended from them all. But I couldn't believe it was just a coincidence that she alone was affected by this. She couldn't be the only one in town descended from all five founders.

No, this felt deliberate.

I needed more information. I needed to find out exactly what was going on here. I needed to find Max Harrington and see exactly how much he knew. I needed to find the artifacts he stole and find out what spells he was using them for.

Abigail made Ella a fresh cup of tea. As she drank, the lights flickered back on. I sank into a chair, rubbing my temples.

"I should go home and sleep," Ella groaned. "I feel awful."

"No, you'll stay right here," Abigail said firmly. "I don't have any guests right now, so I'll make up a room for you. Just sit there and relax. Harper can lend you some pajamas. The two of you are practically the same size."

"I'll help you," I volunteered.

Abigail nodded. As we were making up the room, I saw the worry heavy on Abigail's face, too. I wished I could explain to her everything that was going on. But I couldn't share my magic with anyone, even though Abigail had almost found out about it during the Winter Festival. If she hadn't hit her head, she'd know everything right now.

"Do you have any clues of who's behind the thefts?" Abigail asked me.

I shook my head. "I think it must have to do with the history of Moonhaven, but I don't know what to do."

"You should start where the first building in Moonhaven was constructed. Oh, it's just an empty spot of land now, but Ella knows where it is. She'll be well enough in the morning to take you out there," Abigail said, sounding distracted.

"I don't think it's a good idea to take Ella out anywhere in her condition."

Abigail shook her head. "Nonsense. Getting fresh air will be good for her. Besides, I'm sure once the equinox passes, this strange cold snap will disappear."

The equinox. It was only two days away. A chill washed over me as I realized what this meant. The Spring Equinox was a powerful time for magic. If I couldn't undo the spell on Ella by them, it might be too late.

I had to have Ella with me, so I could counter the spell as soon as I figured out how and why it was placed.

Otherwise, Moonhaven might lose her forever.

## 4

# ANCESTRAL WHISPERS

The next morning, I woke up to good news and bad news. The good news—Ella was feeling much better. She had a spring to her step and the occasional sniffle was the only sign she was still sick. The bad news —the power lines all throughout Moonhaven had gone dead.

There was no apparent reason for it, no damage that anyone could find. People grumbled about it, but to me it was clear what was happening. Magic. Whatever spell was being used was growing more powerful as we got closer to the equinox. I hoped that Ella feeling better meant she was resistant to the magic, but I didn't have much time to figure it all out.

"Ella and I are going to the site where the first building in Moonhaven was built," I told Liam during our morning walk. The air was bitterly cold, and I wished I'd brought a scarf with me.

The cellphone towers were still working, thank goodness. But who knew how long that would last?

"What do you hope to find there?" he asked me.

"I'm not sure," I admitted, turtling into my coat. "But if the thief is obsessed with Moonhaven history, maybe they've been there, too?"

Liam nodded. "Sound thinking. Just be careful."

"Have you found any more evidence indicating Max Harrington is part of this?" I asked him.

"Yesterday, he stopped by the museum and told David he shouldn't be so worried about the break-ins. I'm not sure if that's suspicious or just socially unaware," Liam said, shaking his head. The wind picked up, bringing with it a bite of frost. "You and Ella be careful out there today."

"We will," I promised.

·⸱⸱•♦•⸱·

The spot where the first building of Moonhaven had been erected was several miles out of town. It had been built by Herbert Sinclair; later, when the Whitmans took control politically and financially, they moved the town lines to where it was today. Everything was written out on a plaque in front of the raised stone edges where the foundation had once been.

"It's strange that there's not more snow around here," Ella said as she stood in the middle of where the building had once been. "Look, there's even fresh grass here."

I crouched, touching the ground. Within the foundation of the building, it was clear of snow and growing green. Strange. I glanced at Ella; her back was to me, so I turned my hand over and whispered a spell for my scouting winds. They spread out around me, rustling over the fresh grass—

I sensed the trap just before it sprung. I shouted and lunged for Ella, but as soon as I grabbed her, a rush of magic sprang up from the ground. Bright lights blinded me. Ella cried out, clutching at me.

Then everything was dark. My heart echoed in my ears as I gasped for breath. I still held onto Ella. We both trembled.

"What was that?" she whispered. "I think I've gone blind."

Her words echoed strangely. The chilly air was warmer, much warmer, and as I pulled in a deep breath to calm myself, I caught the scent of... minerals? Damp soil? I fumbled in my pocket and pulled out my cell phone. The screen lit up, illuminating the surrounding area.

Ella's face glowed in the light from the phone. She looked around and her jaw dropped. "Are we in a cave?"

I went to open the flashlight of my phone only for my stomach to drop. With the power outage, it hadn't charged. I only had about five percent left. I needed to save the power to call for help when we got out of here.

I turned it off, and Ella whimpered. "We need light."

"I know." I reached for her hand and squeezed it.

It wouldn't do us any good to stay in here, lost in the darkness. But I had to conserve the power. Which meant I only had one choice left. My stomach quivered as I took a deep breath.

"Ella?"

"Harper?"

"I'm going to do something... and I need you to stay calm, okay?"

Ella's hands tightened around my arm. "Don't leave me!"

In response, I held my hand out palm-up. I summoned my flames and a flickering white light sprang to life in my palm. It cast off a brighter, warmer glow than the phone had, completely illuminating the area around us.

Ella released me and jumped back with a yelp. "How are you doing that?"

"It won't hurt you," I said anxiously. "I know this is strange, but you have to stay calm, okay? I'll explain everything, I promise."

Ella backed away from me, her eyes locked on the flame in my palm.

"Ella... I'm a witch," I told her. My voice trembled as I spoke. "We were transported here by a spell that was cast over the old Sinclair site. I don't know exactly what happened, but I'm sure that everything happening here has to do with magic. The thefts at the museum, the cold snap we're dealing with... everything."

"I must be having a fever dream," Ella murmured, pressing her hand to her forehead.

I waited for her to decide what she was going to do. Thoughts of revealing myself had flitted through my head before, but I'd never told anyone. Even as a child, the knowledge that I could never reveal my secret had been too powerful for me to ignore.

Right now, I felt like I might end up at the bottom of a lake with cement shoes. Not that I believed Ella would hurt me, but I'd broken the cardinal rule... What would the consequences be?

Ella shook her head hard. "Let's look around."

Well, at least she wasn't freaking out. I inspected our surroundings. Beneath our feet was a map of the town. As I kneeled to get a closer look at it, light flooded the cave. I flinched as my eyes strained.

Ella stood next to a camping lantern that cast off enough light to see the entire room clearly. I extinguished my flame, staring at it with low spirits. So if I had only kept my cellphone on long enough to take a better look around, I wouldn't have had to reveal myself to Ella.

"It looks like someone lives out here," Ella said. A camping cot was set up along one wall, with a propane stove, a package of bottled water, and other gear next to it.

"They carved a map of the town into the floor," I said, standing. As I turned in a slow circle, I nodded. "This is where our thief has been holding out. Look. There's the handkerchief, teacup, kettle, iron, and plow from the museum."

"Why would they take all this just to hide it in a cave?" Ella wondered aloud.

I stepped over to the kettle and frowned. "Ella, look at this. This kettle belonged to Herbet Sinclair, right? And it's put right where his original house was built."

Ella frowned and hurried over to the plow. "This is where the Mercer family built their first house."

She stooped and picked up a piece of paper.

"He must have found where the original structures were and brought these items here to perform a spell," I murmured.

"Harper?"

I turned back to Ella.

"This is Max's writing. We were researching..." She held the paper out to me, then dug her hands into her honey-brown hair. "It only says 'center of the ley lines' and then 'net.' What does this mean?"

"Ley lines are alignments of magical currents within the earth's surface," I told her, bending to the map again. "We know the Whitmans had magic, and if Max Harrington is a witch, then it's likely he inherited his magic books from his ancestry."

Ella's eyes were round as saucers as she stared at me.

I laid my hand on the map. "Maybe the other families were magical as well. If they were…"

I nudged a little magic into it. All the lines lit up. The roads glowed pale blue, the buildings green. And over it all, connecting the five spots where the original structures were built, were the golden ley lines. It formed a net over the town.

"Just what I thought. These are where the ley lines run," I told her, straightening. "By building on these spots, the founding families created a net of magic over the town. They would have been able to use it for protection or to make the weather better for crops. Liam said that Moonhaven is much more mild than the surrounding area."

"Then… then something went wrong?" Ella asked incredulously. "To make it turn cold like this?"

"They fought over land and power. So, they lost the connection to each other… and during the Winter Festival, Percival Whitman did more than just attack David," I explained. "He called on ancestral magic to do so. The net must have caught it and amplified it, even after he was jailed."

"How do we break it, then?"

I winced as I turned to her. "This part is where things get weird."

Ella frowned at me. "I'm not sure how it can get weirder."

"The spell has focused on you. You're not sick because the town is cold… the town is cold because you're sick. The net didn't dispel the spell over the town. It focused it on you, the living descendant of the five people who put it into place four hundred years ago."

"I…" She looked horrified, and I couldn't blame her. "But… all these things…"

"I don't know why he did this. What he hopes to get from it," I said, shaking my head. "Liam already suspected Max Harrington was behind the museum thefts. And with this," I lifted the paper with his writing on it. "It's proof. He used magic to steal all these things."

Ella stiffened. To my surprise, her eyes flashed with anger. "Max is my friend. He would never hurt me. I'd sooner believe you were doing this."

I stepped back, hurt.

"And I don't believe you're behind it, either," Ella said, softening again. "But I can't believe Max has anything to do with it. I can't believe any of it... If my ancestors had magic, why don't I?"

"Magic isn't inherited, it's taught. I could teach you how to use magic," I said. "But it's passed on from parent to child. Only, some people decide not to teach their children. Ever since the witch trials, we've been more and more secretive. A lot of knowledge was lost. I don't even know if Percival was taught magic as a child or found the rituals later in life."

Ella rubbed her eyes, then sighed. "This really is all too much for me to understand. But are you sure it's because I'm a descendant of all of them?"

"I can't see another reason."

"My coffee shop." She pointed at the map. "It's where the first Town Hall was built."

I followed where she was pointing. All the ley lines of the area converged into a central spot... right on her coffee shop. I stared hard, watching the pulsing golden lights. If that was where Town Hall had once been... the bell was taken for a reason. These things were taken for a reason.

Ella was certain Max wouldn't hurt her.

"Oh," I whispered.

"What is it?"

"I think I know what's really happening... but we have to get out of here," I said, rushing to grab Ella's hand. "We have little time."

# 5

## THE EQUINOX RITUAL

Ella's teeth were chattering as Liam put a blanket around her shoulders. He reached into the cruiser for a second one for me, but I shook my head.

"Ella needs it more than I do."

She was so exhausted that she didn't protest. Liam helped her into the backseat, where she buckled herself in and promptly sagged against the backrest. I threw my arms around Liam, burying my face into his puffy jacket.

"I was worried I'd given you the wrong directions," I told him.

Liam hugged me back tightly. "What happened?"

I sighed. When Ella and I had navigated out of the cave, I'd only had enough battery life on my phone to give Liam a quick call. I wasn't sure how I was going to explain the whole magical transportation part of things.

"We found a cave with the things that were stolen from the museum," I said as we got into the car. The heat was blowing, warming up my frigid fingers. Liam drove as I continued, "And Ella found a piece of paper with Max Harrington's handwriting on it."

"It wasn't him," Ella insisted sleepily from the back.

Snow drifted down from the sky. I peered at the dark gray clouds in worry. Everything seemed so still and silent... and Ella falling asleep like this could be just from exhaustion, or it could be the spell kicking up another notch.

"How did you find the cave?" Liam asked.

"Tracks in the snow."

Liam glanced at me, his expression frustrated, but didn't search me long. He turned back to the road.

I cleared my throat. "But Max's handwriting proves it was him, right?"

"It's evidence, not proof of anything," Liam reminded me. "And it doesn't say why he's doing any of this."

"Max isn't behind it," Ella said again. "He's my friend. He would never."

I chewed my lip. That was precisely why he was doing it. Hadn't Abigail told me to find the heart of the thief? That was exactly it. Max Harrington loved Ella. It didn't matter if it was a romantic or platonic love—what mattered was that he loved her and wanted to save her.

The only thing was, I couldn't tell Liam any of this. He'd never understand, even if he believed it.

"We need to get to the coffee shop right away," I said.

Liam glanced in the rearview mirror at Ella and nodded. I leaned back, twisting the seat belt in my hands. Ironic that Ella named the shop 'Ella's Wheel' when it was the hub of the ley lines. I wondered how she had got it. Was it inherited or had she bought the place? Did she rent it? How deeply her connection ran would impact how to break the spell laying over her.

"Are we almost there?" Ella asked in a thin voice. She slumped over with a sudden sigh, and my heart jumped.

"Ella?" I called.

Nothing.

Liam's hands tightened on the steering wheel. "She needs a hospital."

"No."

"What are you—she needs a doctor!" Liam shouted incredulously.

I twisted in my seat, sticking my fingers through the cage-like barrier that separated the back from the front. Ella's breathing was deep. Her cheeks were pink, her body relaxed. She looked like she was sleeping soundly.

"We need to get to the coffee shop," I repeated.

"Harper—"

I twisted around again. "Liam, trust me. This is like the Winter Festival all over again. Doctors won't be able to help her. We need to get to the coffee shop. It's where Max is."

Liam's jaw clenched. A muscle ticked in his forehead, but he turned off the main road, twisting through the streets until we got to the coffee shop. Once we were there, I jumped from the cruiser and rushed inside. Max Harrington laid on the floor, his face white. Beneath him was a crudely drawn picture of the map, much like what we'd seen in the cave. Only, instead of the artifacts marking the spots where the original buildings were, there were photocopied portraits of the five founders.

I dropped to my knees next to him, checking his pulse. It was erratic and weak, and his skin was frosty. Beneath his fingers was a picture of him and Ella as children.

"What's going on?" Liam demanded from the doorway.

I turned and gasped. Ella was standing beside him. Soft, wavering, looking confused... Liam looked to where she was but didn't see her. Of course he didn't. It was only her spirit here, the same sort of flickering way I'd seen David Blackwood's spirit during the Winter Festival.

"Ella?"

I whirled to find Max's spirit standing nearby. He flickered, unstable, the same way Ella was. My heart jack rabbited in my chest. Their spirits had distended from their bodies. It wouldn't take much for the tethers that kept them alive to snap and kill them both.

"Ella, I'm sorry," Max said, sounding like he was coming from a far distance. "I thought I could transfer the curse to me. I thought I could save you."

"Harper!" Liam strode forward and grabbed my shoulders, breaking me from my growing horror. "What is going on?"

"Bring Ella in here," I blurted.

He opened his mouth to argue.

"Please," I begged. "Bring her in here. I don't have much time. Trust me."

Liam screwed his eyes shut. He hesitated, and I held my breath. I couldn't do this without him. Forget about keeping magic a secret. This was about the lives of two people, not to mention the fate of the whole town.

"I need you," I whispered.

His eyes opened, full of determination. "You'll owe me an explanation."

He was off before I could answer. I arranged the photocopied portraits on the floor, whispering a spell to adhere each one to the map. A bell tolled in the distance as Liam brought Ella in. I had him lay her down next to Max and pressed their hands together while laying the picture of the two of them right over where the coffee shop was on the map.

"Give me your hand and close your eyes," I told Liam.

His fingers were calloused and his grip firm, but the warmth of his hand gave me hope. I held out my other hand, summoning my revealing winds. They whipped around us. Liam gasped, his eyes still tightly shut. The bell rang harder, louder; the sound echoing through the coffee shop.

So this is where the bell went when Max stole it. He returned it to the spot where it had hung in Town Hall four hundred years ago.

A shimmering tangle of red lines appeared over the map, wrapping Max and Ella up in a twisting net that grew tighter even as I watched. They weren't crisscrossed in the same pattern as the ley lines on the map, though—this net was the spell. It shivered as it tightened, edges curling up and then laying flat again like an octopus.

I released Liam's hand and raced forward as a new rope crawled over their bodies. It twisted in my hand like a snake when I grabbed it. I wrestled it back to the spot where it started from, grunting with the effort. When I touched the raw ends together, it disappeared.

"It's nearing the twelfth stroke," Liam called as the bell tolled again.

My heart stopped. Twelfth stroke. It wasn't anywhere near twelve, be that midnight or midday, but the bell didn't care. We were close enough to the equinox. Max's interference must have sped up the process of it all.

"Help me," I said.

Liam opened his eyes and gasped. "What—"

"We need to get them free of the light," I panted, struggling with the next rope. "Hurry! Please!"

Liam sprang into action. He rushed forward, grabbing onto the rope I struggled with. He planted his feet as he helped me pull it back, yanking relentlessly as I detangled it from the others. Slowly, one by one, we released the net. The ropes still in place shriveled, tightening on Ella and Max.

The last one was across their necks. It wrapped around, wriggling like a snake wanting to strangle them. I lunged and grabbed one side while Liam caught the other side.

The bell tolled twelve and an awful crashing filled the coffee shop. The ceiling burst open, sending wooden shrapnel everywhere. The heavy thing fell directly toward Liam. I screamed but had no time to summon my winds. It struck him, sending him flying, before it crushed the brew bar and rolled toward Max and Ella.

I leaped forward, the rope still gripped in one hand as I braced myself. It knocked into me, sending me stumbling backward, but the bell rolled to a stop before it crushed them. The rope in my hand disappeared and everything fell silent.

Ella groaned. She and Max were both stirring, looking drained and confused.

I rushed to Liam. He lay motionless. Blood soaked through his hair and I ripped off my sweater to press to the gash on his scalp. His skin was pale, but he was breathing visibly.

"Max, call the ambulance," I yelled over my shoulder.

He groaned in response. "What happened?"

"Call the ambulance," I repeated.

"Give me your phone," Ella said. She called the ambulance while I held onto Liam, shaking with fear. How serious was this? What if the bell had done permanent damage?

Max crawled over beside me. He pushed a book toward me; it was bound in green leather with the image of standing stones on the front. His gaze was still confused, but he silently put his hands over mine, pressing down on Liam's injury to prevent more bleeding.

"I don't know what to do," he rasped. "Ella has to perform the ritual."

# 6

## REBIRTH OF TRUTH

My finger pressed to the page, underlining the words describing the ritual I was meant to do. Ella wrapped her arms around herself, shivering despite the warmth of the room. I hurried back to her side and pulled her into the center of the map. The portraits were still in place, so I backed off the map.

"Hold your hand out and touch the bell," I instructed.

She did so; her face rapidly turning more ashen. Outside, the wind howled, driving snow into the window with such force it was almost hail. The sky turned dark.

Holding both my hands upward, I summoned my winds. They whipped through the room, picking up the portraits.

"The curses of those who have gone before are broken," I called. "Release her by the blood of her ancestors."

Outside, the wind died suddenly and the hail-like snow turned to a soft, pattering rain. The sink behind the brew bar streamed with water and the giant hole in the ceiling disappeared, along with the bell. The portraits disappeared in green flames and all went still.

Ella pulled in a deep breath, the color returning to her face. She stood straight, no longer trembling. "Is it done?"

I nodded, my shoulders slumping. "It's done. You're free."

The sound of sirens took our attention. Ella hurried to the door to talk to the paramedics while I returned to Liam, kneeling next to him. He was even paler than before, but his breathing was still even. I checked his pulse and was relieved when I found it strong.

The paramedics took Liam away, leaving Ella, Max, and me to clean up the rest of the coffee shop. While the hole in the ceiling had fixed itself, the lights were still scattered all over the floor, along with giant chunks of plaster.

"Where do you think the bell went?" Max asked, subdued.

"That depends. Are you the one that took it?"

Max shook his head. "I knew it would come back here with the spell. I thought it wouldn't come until tomorrow. I thought I had a day left to fix it."

He bowed his head, his shoulders slumping.

Ella stepped up beside him and touched his elbow. "So you were doing all of this to save me? When I didn't even know something was wrong?"

"Yeah. After what happened at the Winter Festival, I thought that the things my grandfather used to tell me were real after all. I've been reading everything I could find, but..." He lifted his head and stared at me, his brow furrowed. "But I don't know as much as you do."

"You're not a witch. Not yet, at least," I said awkwardly. "You tried to take the spell off Ella and put it on yourself."

Ella gasped.

"That's where you went wrong. You don't have the ancestry she does, so it only made the curses laid on the Harrington line stronger," I explained.

Max let out a shaky breath.

"It worked out this time, but don't use magic without proper guidance again," I warned him. "Not only is it dangerous to you, but it's dangerous to all of us. You two might not be witches, might not have the training, but the witch hunters won't care."

Ella's eyes turned round. "Witch hunters?"

I shivered. "I'll tell you about them later. Just know that they exist. And for that reason, you must tell no one what happened here. Nobody can know."

Both of them nodded seriously. I hoped that they'd take my warnings to heart. My hands shook with anxiety as I grabbed a broom. In a single day, I'd revealed my magic to not one, but three people. What would the repercussions be?

"You should get to the hospital to check on Liam," Ella said.

I flinched. My stomach twisted as my blood ran even colder. I was trying to distract myself from the worry, hoping that if I kept busy, I might skip the awful waiting. What would I do if he didn't recover? There was so much blood.

"Harper." Ella put her arms around me as I crumpled inward. "You should be there when he wakes up."

My chest hurt, but I nodded. "I can't drive myself."

"We'll drive you," Max said. "Then maybe swing by the museum and see if the bell came back."

Ella smiled at him. "Maybe even go out to that cave and take back everything you stole?"

He blushed and ducked his head.

Outside, nearly all the snow had been melted by the rain already. The yards, once hidden, were vibrant green. There were even a few flowers already growing here and there. I sighed; this meant the spell was truly broken.

Ella would be okay.

Max sighed as well as we got into the car. "I want to help Moonhaven. There are so many deep hurts caused by the disputes of the past. I wish there was more I could do."

"We'll keep working on that," I told him. "Moonhaven is a powerfully magical place. But you have to be ready to face punishment for your thefts, Max. I don't think Liam will turn a blind eye to this."

My stomach cramped again. Liam would get better. He had to. Which meant, of course, he was going to throw the book at Max... and demand answers from me. I wasn't sure what I'd tell him yet, but I'd think of something. The truth was always a good idea. There certainly were no lies that would trick him after what he saw.

As we drove, Ella leaned forward and wrapped her arms around me. "I think I understand."

"Understand?" I repeated, confused.

"Why you didn't tell me? I mean, obviously, there's stuff to it I don't know. Witch hunters and all that... but even without that, I understand why you wouldn't tell me you're a witch. It must be lonely, having a secret like that... something that, if the truth got out, you don't know if you'd be safe or not."

Tears flooded my eyes. That was exactly what I felt.

"I will always be your friend, Harper," Ella promised me. "Always."

Sniffing, I nodded.

They dropped me off at the front of the hospital and made me promise to tell them as soon as I had any updates. I headed into the hospital, my steps heavy. To my surprise, I found Abigail was already in Liam's room when I was brought there. Her cloud of gray hair was loose around her shoulders and her eyes were closed.

I never would have figured out what was going on with Max if it weren't for her cryptic advice two days ago. It seemed so much longer than that.

She opened her eyes and smiled at me as I sank into the chair next to her. "I was wondering when you'd get here."

"How is he?" I asked, looking anxiously at him.

His breathing was even, and his color better than it had been in the coffee shop. His head was bandaged, and an IV dripped into his arm. I laced my fingers together as I searched the room for any sign of how bad it was.

"He has a concussion and needed stitches to close up that gash in his scalp, but he'll be fine," Abigail said.

I slumped back in my chair, covering my face. Relief swept through me as I struggled to breathe evenly. Part of me wanted to cry in sheer relief.

Abigail rubbed my back. "I just sent Ella a text before you came in. Do you know what happened?"

I shook my head, unable to talk about it. We'd told the paramedics that the light fixture had broken free and struck Liam's head. I hoped it was a good enough explanation to stick.

"How do you know so much about what goes on in this town?" I blurted, looking up at Abigail. She always seemed to know what was going on... was it just a coincidence?

Abigail shrugged. "Moonhaven holds many secrets. When you're old enough, you see them much clearer."

Before I could ask her what she meant, Liam groaned.

I leaned forward, grasping his hand. "Liam?"

His eyes opened and squished back shut. "Ugh. I haven't had a hangover like this since... ever."

I laughed shakily.

Abigail patted my shoulder. "I'll go get the doctors."

"Doctors?" Liam opened his eyes again. He squinted blearily at me.

I rubbed my thumb over his knuckles. "You don't think I'd leave you after hitting your head like that, do you?"

Liam reached up to touch his head, a bewildered expression on his face. "Did I slip on the ice or something?"

"No, you—" I cut myself off. Slip on the ice? My heart pounded. "What do you remember last?"

"We were walking, and you were talking about the spring equinox."

I straightened. "Liam... that was two days ago. You hit your head in the coffee shop. Don't you remember?"

His gaze met mine. Confusion swam in his eyes. I held my breath as I stared back. So this meant he had no memory of the last two days? No memory of the ritual we'd performed to save Ella and Max? I should be relieved, but I... I couldn't tell if I was. Or if some part of me was upset that he didn't know my secret.

It was good news for Max, though. So long as he and Ella returned the items he stole without being caught, it meant Liam wouldn't keep looking for the thief.

"Harper?" Liam asked me. He sounded... vulnerable.

I squeezed his hand. "It's all going to be fine. You're okay, and I'll tell you what happened these last two days."

Not all of it, though. Never all of it. I forced a smile at him and kissed his cheek, surprising myself.

"I'm staying with you," I told him. "I'm going to take care of you."

Liam smiled back. The tension melted from his body, and he closed his eyes again. "Thank you."

Butterflies swarmed my stomach. But along with them were the seeds of guilt for the lies I was already preparing for him. I had no choice. The number one rule of being a witch was to tell nobody.

But Liam was alive. He wasn't badly injured. I squeezed his hand again. Everything was going to be just fine.


The End
Did you enjoy *Equinox Enigma*?
Please consider rating it on Amazon, Goodreads, or Bookbub.
Reviews help me reach new readers.
Read **May Day Murmurs**, the next story in the **Mystic Moonhaven Mysteries**.


Have you read the *Jane and Kennedy Daniels Mysteries*, the *Annie Archer Paranormal Mysteries*, the *Wilma Wade Holiday Mysteries,* the *Mike and Maddie Mysteries,* or the *Pine Grove Mysteries*?

# 1

## MAY DAY MYSTERIES

I hummed along with the cheerful music Ella had blasting out of the speakers of her coffee shop, Ella's Wheel. I leaned back on the short ladder, careful to keep my balance, and scrutinized the paper flower bouquet I'd just pinned into place. The bright colors popped against the neutral-toned wall and I nodded in satisfaction.

"I need some of the red ribbon," I told Detective Liam Ashford, who stood at the base of my ladder.

"Oh, Harper, that looks beautiful," Abigail said.

He handed me the ribbon. Liam, Abigail Thorne, and I were helping Ella Grace, my best friend, decorate her coffee shop for the May Day festival. I'd lived in Moonhaven for almost a year and a half now, but it would only be my second May Day here. I'd never lived anywhere where it was celebrated before.

Here in Moonhaven, it was a big deal. There were pie baking competitions, various athletic challenges—featuring classics like potato sack races—and, of course, the May Day dance, led by the May Queen.

I loved it all. It helped that May Day fell either on or close to Beltane, which was something that I and my parents celebrated when they were still alive. Not all witches do, but we had Gaelic ancestry, which had been passed down for a long time in our family. I was looking forward to my own private protection rites during the peak of the moon.

"Don't you think that's a bit of overkill?" Liam asked me, drawing me out of my thoughts. He frowned up at my work with a critical eye. "It looked better without the ribbon."

"You can't have May Day without ribbons," I protested.

Liam set the box of decorations he was holding for me aside. "Let me get up there and show you what I mean."

I shook my head firmly. "You're still on leave because of your head injury. How about we not risk you getting dizzy and falling off the ladder?"

Liam sighed. "I don't get dizzy anymore. The doctors say I'm almost fully healed. I get the occasional headache now and that's it."

"Liam." I climbed down the ladder. "It's my fault you were hurt. I just don't want you to get worse because of me, too."

Liam's expression softened. He opened his mouth to reply, but before he could, the front door opened. Anabel Marley, this year's May Queen, swept in wearing a pioneer-era gingham print dress with a frilly white apron. A wide-brimmed straw hat perched on her head as she beamed at everyone in the shop.

"Anabel, aren't you beautiful!" Ella exclaimed, hurrying forward. She hugged Anabel—Ella was pretty much best friends with everyone in Moonhaven.

"Thank you, darling," Anabel replied, beaming. She waved a handful of pamphlets in the air. "I was just stopping by to see if I could leave these here. As May Queen, I've decided to start a fundraiser to help protect the old wishing well. It's getting so run down and needs to be restored if it's going to last for future generations."

I headed over, interested. "I haven't heard anything about a wishing well in Moonhaven."

"It's been there forever," Anabel gushed. "And it's said that on certain days, if you flip a coin into it, it'll grant you a wish. I wish at it every year and I always get what I wished for. And this year, I'm wishing that the community will pitch in and let us restore it!"

Ella laughed. "A selfless wish indeed!"

"Well, since I lost the mayor election, I might as well focus on the community, right?" Anabel asked with a toothy grin.

"I'll put the pamphlets out when I open up for customers tomorrow," Ella promised. "Harper, do you want some for your bookshop?"

"Sure. I love to see old things restored," I replied.

I took a handful of the pamphlets and stored them in my purse. Anabel gushed her thanks for a bit before leaving in as much of a whirlwind as she arrived. All the while, Abigail and Liam had continued working. They were almost done putting up the flowers at eye level. Ella and I were responsible for the higher ones.

"Thank you, dear," Abigail told him, patting his shoulder as he returned the box to a table. "Doesn't that look beautiful?"

Liam nodded, looking distracted. He glanced upward toward the ceiling as though nervous. I winced. It was three months ago now that a series of magical events had ended up with the old town bell crashing through that ceiling. We told him it was falling lights, but the truth was that the bell smashed him in the head before it disappeared back to its resting place in the museum.

"If that well was real, I'd wish to be back at work already," he grumbled. "I hate sitting around doing nothing."

"Yes, hanging out with me in my bookstore is nothing," I teased.

"That's not what I meant, Harper," he protested, blushing.

I tapped my chin, smirking at him. "I think it is. After all, I peddle hooky nonsense, don't I?"

His blush deepened as I reminded him of the first thing he'd ever told me about my bookstore. That was back when I was only selling books on magical things. Witchcraft, occultism, crystals, the whole shebang. I'd wanted to somehow make magic more normal.

I hated hiding my magic from the world. I'd hoped that if there was enough commercialism for it, maybe one day I and the other witches wouldn't have to hide. These days I had more diversity since I wasn't making as much profit as I needed to stay afloat.

If the head injury hadn't wiped his memory clean, Liam wouldn't be calling my shop hooky—he'd know it was true.

"I still don't believe any of that stuff, but I'm sorry for saying it," Liam said.

Abigail spoke sharply. "You can apologize without reminding us how much you don't believe."

I jumped and stared at her. Abigail was usually so even-tempered. What caused her to snap like that?

Ella saved the day, slipping between the two of them. "Why don't you two see the well for yourselves? Wouldn't hurt to make a wish."

Abigail sighed, her gaze distant as though she was remembering something unpleasant. "Wishes are all well and good, but sometimes we get more than we bargained for."

I frowned at her, but as I tried to decide whether to ask, she shook her head and smiled. It seemed strained but genuine. "You two should go off. Ella and I will finish up around here."

I hesitated. There was far more magic in Moonhaven than I'd realized when I first moved here. In fact, it looked the five founding families all had magic, too. It wouldn't surprise me if there were plenty of other witches around here, keeping their secrets as assuredly as I was keeping mine. It was drilled into us over and over—let no one know.

Just three months ago, I'd broken that rule. Ella now knew about my magic. Unlike Liam, she hadn't gotten smashed in the head and forgot about it... but I had to admit, there was a great deal of relief in being able to share.

Ella wasn't about to tell anyone, either. Her coffee shop might be the hub of the rumor mill, but she knew when to keep secrets.

The wishing well could be real. There were many magical ley lines here in Moonhaven, and it was likely that some of them could intersect the well, giving it enough magic to grant wishes. If that was the case, then I'd like to investigate. And considering that Abigail's sudden change in mood happened when the well was brought up, maybe she knew more than she was letting on.

"Oh, shoot!" Ella groaned as she pawed through a box. "I'm out of yellow ribbons."

"We'll go get some," Liam offered.

"Thanks."

Liam and I headed out. While we were driving to the store, he sighed heavily. It sounded so defeated that I winced.

"You okay?" I asked.

"I want to go to the well. Don't give me that look," he said, shaking his head. "Keep your eyes on the road."

I closed my mouth and focused back on where I was driving. "I didn't think you'd actually be interested."

"Normally, I wouldn't. But I feel like I'm missing something... and at this point, I'm willing to do anything to get it back," he said, his blue eyes dark with unspoken emotion.

I chewed my lip. Was there something wrong with him? Did the blow to his head cause worse damage than he'd told me? Or was it because he had seen magic for himself and was now unconsciously picking up on the fact that he ought to know more than he did?

"What did you lose?" I asked him.

"Not sure."

"But you have to have some idea," I protested.

Liam shook his head. "Your guess is as good as mine."

But there was an edge to his voice that made me doubt his words. Was there more going on with him? I bit my lips together and didn't push. He'd tell me what was going on when he was ready... right?

## 2

# THE WHISPERING WELL

Abigail stopped by the bookstore as I was getting ready to head out the next day. I hadn't seen her that morning before I left the B&B and was surprised at how tired she looked. Usually, Abigail was full of vigor and vitality.

"So, are you and Liam planning to go out to that well?" Abigail asked.

My eyebrows drew together as I nodded. "Yeah. I'm closing up the shop, and then we're going to head out before we need to get back to finish preparing for the May Day dance."

"I see." Abigail wrapped her arms around herself. That same distant look came to her face, and I got the impression that she was upset by this news.

I didn't get it. Yesterday, she encouraged Liam and me to check it out. So why did she seem like she thought it was a bad idea now? Had something happened? I wracked my brain but couldn't think of any reason she would change her mind like this.

"Is there a reason we shouldn't?" I asked.

Abigail hesitated, then shrugged. "Some things are not worth digging into. Moonhaven has been unstable lately..." Her gaze latched onto me with a razor-sharp focus. "You need to be more careful."

A chill caused goosebumps to rise over my arms. Did she know something? Abigail seemed to know everything that happened in Moonhaven. Even more than Ella, although Abigail kept things closer to the vest. So was there something happening? What did she know?

"What do you mean?" I asked.

"I mean, first there was that business with David Blackwood being kidnapped, then poor Adam Carter's accident, and that entire business three months ago with the bell disappearing from the museum only to reappear a few days later." Abigail shook her head. "It's not right. Just be careful."

I reached for her hand and squeezed it reassuringly, touched by her concern. "I will be," I promised.

Liam pulled up in his car and I stepped out of the bookstore, locking it behind me. Abigail waved and returned to the B&B while I got into the car.

"What do you have there?" Liam asked, nodding toward my hand.

I shoved the paper into my pocket. "Nothing."

Truthfully, it was a map of the ley lines that ran through Moonhaven. I'd gotten it from Max Harrington during the Spring Equinox and thought it might come in handy here.

The well was overgrown with plants. Grasses tangled with weeds around the base, and the wooden winch sitting over it was broken and sagged with rot. Stones crumbled out here and there. All in all, it looked more like a horror well than a wishing well.

I stooped and cleared out some weeds growing around it. I caught hold of a dandelion that had taken root between two stones in the well itself, but two stones came with it when I pulled. After that, I decided leaving the cleanup to Anabel Marley's fundraiser was better.

"This should be covered up," Liam grumbled as he walked around the well. "It's a danger if anyone was to fall into it. It should be filled in," he added, amending his previous statement.

As he studied the well, I pulled the map from my pocket. The well lay at a cross point of two ley lines, which indicated that it could be magical. Of course, these things didn't necessarily have to happen, but it was possible that when everything aligned, it really could grant wishes.

I pulled a quarter from my pocket and flipped it into the well. It made no noise, no satisfying plunk. Either the well was deeper than I realized or it had gotten caught in plants or something on the way down.

*Help me know what to do*, I wished.

Liam gave me a look.

"What? You said that you wanted to come here," I pointed out. "I know you don't believe it's a real wishing well. I don't know if I do, either. But it can't hurt, right? Just toss a coin into the well."

His lips twitched as he pulled something from his pocket. "You know, I bet Anabel Marley would be able to pay for at least some of the repairs for this place if she was to troll the well. Generations of people throwing their coins in there... depending on how long it's been a wishing well, there could be some rare and expensive coins down there."

I stepped closer to him as he closed his eyes and tossed the coin into the well. "I lost something I need to get back."

I reached for his hand, wanting to comfort him. "Is it about what happened on the spring equinox?"

His shoulders remained tense as he nodded.

What would I say to him? It wasn't exactly my fault that he'd lost a whole weekend, but I still benefited from it. Not to mention he was only in that situation because of me. I squeezed his hand, my head bowed.

"I wish I could help you," I murmured.

"It's just frustrating, not knowing. Doesn't help that I can't get to work. Ever since I was a kid, I'd watch police procedurals and want to do that. I wanted to protect people," he murmured. Then he ran a hand through his light brown hair, laughing. "And that's another thing. I don't feel like I'm actually protecting people. I can't do anything until after something terrible has happened."

My heart ached for him. "You saved David Blackwood."

Liam shook his head. "I didn't. I got a note telling me where to find him. That's all. He was already in a terrible position, and I couldn't save him."

"You *can't* know everything," I protested. My heart beat harder as I took in the weariness on Liam's face. "And you can't know everything."

"I know. I just wish I could do more."

"You're doing the best you can."

Liam sighed as he squeezed my fingers a little tighter. "Thank you, Harper. I know it must be hard for you to hear me talk like this. I'll be okay."

"I'm here if you want to talk."

He turned to me, his expression softening. The tension released from his shoulders, and his eyes lit up as he gazed at me. "I know. Thank you, Harper. You're a good friend."

We stood for a moment longer, each lost in our own thoughts. Would it be so dangerous if I told him everything about my magic? Ella knew, and nothing bad had happened. I knew there were witch hunters out there still, but I'd never had any personal interactions with them. Only stories told by my parents.

Now that I thought of it, I wasn't sure they'd had personal experiences, either. Was it all just warnings passed from parent to child, and the threat was gone? I knew I couldn't take that risk, but I wanted to tell Liam so badly...

Eventually, he sighed. "We should get back to town."

"Want to hang out tonight?" I asked as we turned back to the car.

"I'll think about it. I might be busy."

Liam opened my door for me. As I slid in, I saw a curled piece of paper on the seat. One was in Liam's seat as well. I grabbed them both and straightened. Liam frowned as I handed him the note that had been on his seat.

"They look like they're old," I said.

The paper was thick and heavy. When I opened mine, the writing inside was thin with several ink splatters, as though it had been written with a feather quill and an unsteady hand.

"What is lost will be found, but what cost will hope be drowned," he read aloud. A heavy frown crossed his face as he turned it over. "What is that supposed to be?"

"You wished you could find what you lost," I pointed out, curling my fist around the note left for me. My heart hammered as I glanced uneasily at the well. I'd never heard of a wishing well granting ominous warnings rather than granting a wish one way or another.

Liam snorted. "What does yours say?"

"Nothing. It's blank."

His eyebrows arched toward his hairline, and then he shrugged. "I guess that's because I said my wish out loud, and you didn't, so they weren't sure what to write for you."

"They?" I asked, confused.

"It's got to be a prank," Liam replied.

"Right. Of course." I slid into the car and shoved the paper into my pocket.

I couldn't tell him he was wrong. My paper wasn't empty but directly related to my silent wish. If I shared it with him, he would be curious about what it meant. I didn't have the wherewithal to come up with a lie about anything I'd want to keep secret that would ultimately be harmless.

I wanted Liam to know about my magic. I'd asked for help. And I got my answer...

Nobody must know.

## 3

# WISHES GONE WRONG

"That happened to me, too."

I looked up from the coffee I'd been staring at to find Mayor Caleb at the end of the booth Liam and I sat at. Ella was sitting next to me, listening to what happened to us at the wishing well. I'd completely zoned out, my head too full of thoughts about Liam and magic to really listen to what was going on around me. It'd been a mistake, apparently.

Not only was the mayor there, but several others as well.

"Me, too," a tall, muscular woman agreed. "I made a wish last week, hoping my boyfriend would propose. I ended up with a note in my jewelry box saying, 'Wedded bliss may hide shadows. Be careful where you shine your light.' It was weird."

Caleb nodded. His normal business jacket was slung over his arm. "Mine was weird, too. Sounded more like a threat than a granted wish."

Liam leaned forward. "We're theorizing that someone is playing some sort of massive prank on the town. We're looking into it."

"Good." Caleb nodded. "I want to see that whispering well shut down forever. The best course of action would be to fill it in."

"You can't mean that," Ella protested, aghast.

I wrinkled my nose. While normally I'd be all for preserving local history, this was one thing I might agree with Caleb about. If the magic in the well had been corrupted, there was a high chance that we could end up with a disaster on our hands. Something must have happened to the well, to change it from granting wishes to offering these warnings.

"It's a danger," Caleb muttered. He shrugged. "But then, we could always fill it up and restore the outer parts."

Ella slumped back, looking unconvinced.

Caleb headed outside. He nearly ran into Max Harrington as he came in. The two dipped their heads at each other, and Max waved to Ella as he headed for the brew bar. He briefly met my eyes and gave me a strained smile before he turned his attention away.

"Excuse me," Ella said.

Liam tapped his fingers against the table, looking distracted.

I rolled my shoulders to loosen them. "What are you thinking?"

"That something is happening in Moonhaven. Prank or not, this feels too important to ignore," Liam said, then gave me a wry smile. "Although that might be because I'm getting more and more anxious to get back to work."

"No, I agree. Something weird is happening," I said. "Though I probably have a little more leaning toward the whole wishing well being an actual wishing well thing, rather than someone carrying out elaborate pranks."

I expected Liam to laugh, but he turned his face away. As his gaze landed on Max and Ella, his eyes darkened.

"You know, I'm still convinced that man was part of those weird thefts at the museum. Maybe he has something to do with this too."

"But everything was returned to the museum."

Liam shrugged. "Does it matter? They were still taken in the first place. And if he's part of this, it means he's escalating."

I shook my head. "I can't believe that Max is behind any of this. He's a good guy. He and Ella are great friends and have been since they were children. No, he doesn't have anything to do with these ominous warnings."

"All I know is that when I got that blow to my head, it made me forget something important," Liam growled.

My heart jumped to my throat. It did—but it had nothing to do with Max and everything to do with me. How could I sit here across from him and pretend like everything was okay when I knew what he'd lost?

I steeled myself. "That has nothing to do with the well, though."

"No. No, I suppose it doesn't."

Guilt hit me in the stomach. It wasn't right for me to keep so much from him... yet the warning from the well echoed the warnings I'd gotten from my parents for as long as I could remember. Nobody can know.

I was relieved when Ella came back to us. She slid into the booth beside me, her brow furrowed. "What are we talking about?"

"The well."

Ella nodded. "Right. Before Caleb interrupted us, I was going to say that I heard someone drowned in the well forty years ago."

I straightened. A death in the well would certainly cause the magic inside to change if the spirit of the deceased was still connected to it somehow. "Who was it?"

"I can't remember his name. But I do know that the police at the time suspected it was murder, but didn't have a solid suspect," Ella offered.

Liam finished his coffee. "I doubt it'll go anywhere, but I'll look at the old reports. Maybe they'll give me a clue."

"Are you sure? You're not supposed to go back to work," I said. My stomach twisted.

"I'm sure. It's not work." He winked at me and headed out.

I watched him go; the knots increasing in my stomach. The coffee shop was empty now except for the dishwasher in the back and Max Harrington still at the brew bar. It was during the time of day when business was quiet, but the emptiness still sent a chill up my spine.

"Harper?" Ella leaned in close, lowering her voice. "Does this have to do with magic?"

"Yeah. The well is at cross points between two ley lines, and if someone drowned in it, then their spirit may have remained attached to the physical location."

Ella chewed her lip. "I was afraid of that. So, there's more you should know. Every forty years, someone drowns. Which means that this year..."

The hairs on my arms stood on end. If this was forty years since the last death, it meant that there would be another victim of the well. My mind raced. Multiple deaths in such a pattern weren't a coincidence. There was something more powerful in the well than I'd realized.

I let out a shaky breath.

"I didn't want to say anything in front of Liam because of the magical connection," Ella whispered. "I'm sure he'll figure it out on his own, though."

I nodded in agreement.

"One last thing." Ella twisted her hands as she glanced at Max's back. He stayed where he was, looking like he was playing on his phone. Only his whole body was stiff and awkward. Clearly, he was only pretending to be uninterested in what was going on behind him. "Max told me he found something out. The first victim of the well? None other than Howard Whitman himself."

I gasped.

Max turned at the sound. His gaze met mine, and he glanced back at his phone. For the three of us trying to be stealthy, we weren't doing an excellent job. My hands tightened around my empty mug as my mind raced.

Howard Whitman had been a witch living in Moonhaven four hundred years ago. He was one of the founding members of the town and had used his magic to kill off members of the Blackwood family until he could claim their land as his. So many of the terrible things that happened in Moonhaven seemed to be traced right back to him!

"The well marked a contested boundary between his property and Laurence Mercer's land," Ella continued. "When Whitman was found dead in the well, everyone suspected it was Laurence. They never had proof so nothing happened to him, but they were convinced."

"It started with him, then," I murmured. "Let me guess. He was forty years old when he died?"

Ella nodded, her eyes wide. "How did you know?"

"Because the well claims a victim every forty years. This is because of him. He left an imprint on the well, causing all of this."

Ella rubbed the back of her neck, shivering. "There's something else. Something worse."

I focused back on her. What could be worse than knowing that this was a four-hundred-year-old curse?

"I do know who the last victim was. And Liam is going to find out soon enough, too." Ella leaned in even closer, lowering her voice. "His name was Owen Cook. And he died in the middle of a dispute with Abigail. Apparently, they were engaged. She broke it off, and there was controversy surrounding the ring."

So that was why Abigail acted so cagey about it all! It must have been so upsetting to be reminded about this. But... if they were in the middle of a dispute, did that mean that Abigail had been a murder suspect forty years ago?

A scream from outside made me nearly jump from my skin. Ella and I both jumped up and rushed outside, Max accompanying us. We crowded out the door to find Anabel Marley standing toe-to-toe with Mayor Caleb Fuller. They were screaming at each other so loudly that I couldn't catch what they were saying.

Until—

"I wish you would disappear and never bother me again!" Anabel shouted.

She spun on her heel and marched away.

But even as she did, I felt a stirring in the air. Magic collating together, focusing. A rush of cold ripped through me as I stared at the mayor. He scoffed and walked the other way, the magic following him.

Anabel's wish was going to come true.

I'd just found the well's next victim.

# DANCING WITH DANGER

My hair was curled and done up in a vaguely Regency style and I wore a loose, flowing summer dress perfect for the warm community hall. It was the night of the May Day dance and the night when the well was going to claim its victim.

"You two keep Caleb here," I whispered to Ella and Max. "He'll be safe after midnight, I'm sure of it."

Ella nodded, her expression fierce and determined. "You be careful."

I hugged her and slipped away. There were plenty of people in the middle of the dance floor already, while most lingered around the edges, chatting and conversing. I quickly spied the fluffy cloud of gray hair I was looking for and made a beeline for Abigail.

"Harper, you look lovely," Abigail said, smiling.

I didn't return it. "I need to talk to you... about Owen Cook."

Abigail's smile disappeared at once. She glanced around, then brushed past me to head outside. My hands shook as I followed her. I didn't like this at all, but I hadn't been able to find out enough about the well on my own. Maybe if I figured out what caused the dispute between her and Owen, I'd be able to figure out why the well chose him forty years ago.

Once we were outside, alone beneath an oak tree, Abigail turned on me. "Why are you asking about him?"

"Please, Abigail. I need to know," I said, hoping that she wouldn't insist on an explanation.

Abigail closed her eyes. Her arms wrapped around her middle. Normally, she was vivacious and full of life. Now, she looked her age. It was a little frightening, if I was honest.

"Owen Cook... I loved him. He breezed into town one day, full of smiles and charm. He listened to me when I told him about my dreams and encouraged me to defy my parents and seek an education. It sounds crazy these days," she said, sighing. "But I was raised by very strict parents who were restrictive about women's roles even considering the times were changing."

She shook her head, her eyes still distant and sad.

"What happened, then?" I asked, moving forward. "I heard you broke your engagement to him."

"He proposed and paid for my grandmother's ring to be resized to use it as my engagement ring. He made sure that I got my inheritance from her, the money that my parents had been controlling... then, all of a sudden, he was cooling his heels. Saying that I needed to reconcile with them before we married."

My stomach hurt. I knew where this was going.

Abigail's eyes grew fiery. "I learned he was stealing my inheritance. He was blowing through all the money I had. He was nothing but a charlatan, so I broke our engagement."

"That must have been so hard," I whispered. "I can't imagine how painful it must have been for you."

"More than painful. My parents had kicked me out, so I was living with Owen. It caused quite a scandal... once I broke it off with him, he threw me out with only the clothes on my back. I had nowhere to go and couldn't even access the money that was rightfully mine. I had to crawl back to my parents and they never let me forget it."

She continued. "I still had my grandmother's ring... and he tried to claim that it should belong to him since he paid for it to be resized."

I gaped. "That's ridiculous!"

"It was, but he was good friends with our judge at the time. I was so worried I'd lose the ring and I was so stressed about everything... I agreed to give up the property that we'd bought with my inheritance if he'd stop fighting for the ring. I kept my promise. He didn't."

My hands clenched, my anger useless. "He sounds like a terrible piece of work!"

Abigail smiled softly. "He was. The only good thing that came from it was that my aunt moved into town. She insisted I move in with her, and it was only then that I felt my real freedom. She was a lawyer and got my inheritance and several belongings back from him.

"Then we went on a massive PR campaign through town," she continued, chuckling. "I worked my butt off. It took months, but eventually, people stopped seeing me as a fallen woman and rather as the victim of a cad. Owen's reputation suffered. He was furious, of course, but we'd won the town over.

"I was voted May Queen that year," Abigail continued. Her shoulders slumped as she shook her head. "While I was performing my charitable duties, someone—I'm sure Owen—broke into my aunt's house. Nobody was home so nobody was hurt, thank goodness. But my grandmother's ring and many other heirlooms were stolen."

I leaned against the oak, pulling my shawl tighter around my shoulders. The night was chilly once we were away from the crowded hall. I processed what Abigail had told me.

With all of this in mind, then why didn't the police think she was a suspect in Owen's death? Not that I thought she was capable of murder, not by a long shot, but with all of her reasons to go after Owen...

"You said you're sure it was Owen. Didn't they catch him?" I asked.

Abigail shook her head. Her gray hair glowed silver beneath the moonlight. "The police could find no proof that he was the one who did it. They didn't care, either. Owen was still friends with that judge, after all."

"That makes a lot of sense," a voice said from among the cars.

I jumped, then relaxed when Liam wove through the vehicles to join us. He nodded toward Abigail. "I'm sorry for eavesdropping."

"It's fine." Abigail waved a hand. "Better than having to tell the whole sordid story twice."

Liam held up an old brown folder. "I've been looking into the report of Owen Cook's death. It's a... interesting case."

The wind picked up, cutting through my thin dress. I shivered and sidled closer to Liam. He took off his jacket and wrapped it around my shoulders. Abigail gave me a knowing smile. I stared back blankly at her—what was she looking at me like that for?

"Owen drowned in the well, but he had a contusion on the back of his head," Liam said. "It could have been caused by him falling in. Or it could have been someone who hit him in the back of the head and pushed him into the well."

"I didn't kill him," Abigail said softly.

Liam's hard expression softened. "I don't think you did, Abigail. Not without a good reason, anyway. Besides, the police found your ring in his pocket. If you'd been the one to do it, you'd have taken it back."

"They found my grandmother's ring?" Abigail demanded, her voice raising. "Why didn't they tell me?"

"I can't answer that. It's been kept at the precinct for forty years as evidence," Liam explained.

"Can I have it back?" Abigail asked, longing clear in her eyes.

"I'm afraid—"

"Look," I interrupted, grabbing Liam's arm. He turned, following my gaze.

Anabel Marley, decked out in the costume jewelry that came with being May Queen, hurried out of the dance. She made a beeline for her car and tore out with squealing brakes. The scent of burnt tires lingered in the air... combining with a sweet, cloying scent of magic. It followed her the same way it had followed Caleb earlier in the day.

"Oh, no," Abigail breathed. "You have to go after her."

"What?" Liam frowned.

I grabbed his hand. "She looked upset and was driving erratically. That's a reason, right?"

My heart slammed into my ribs as I pulled him toward my car. Had I been wrong? Was it Anabel, not Caleb, that the well had latched onto?

We tore out after her, following... right to the well. The feeling of magic grew stronger and stronger the closer we got to it. Faint golden lights flickered along the horizon. The ley lines? I wasn't sure—but I knew one thing. Something terrible was going to happen unless we stopped it!

We arrived at the well to find Anabel leaning over the side of it. Her hands clutched at the old stones as she sobbed, her tears dripping into the well.

Liam and I jumped out of the car. But even as we did so, a shadow emerged from the nearby trees. I shouted and Anabel lifted her head—but it was too late. The shadow knocked into her, sending her careening into the well. It bolted back for the woods.

Liam chased after the shadow, shouting, "Police! Stop!"

I raced to the edge of the well. Several stones had dislodged and fallen in after Anabel. "Anabel?" I cried. My voice echoed back toward me. "Anabel!"

There was no answer.

## 5

# THE MAY QUEEN'S SECRET

Bile rose in the back of my throat as I leaned over the crumbling rock wall. Moonlight glinted off the opposite wall, but I couldn't see down far enough to tell where Anabel had dropped to. I reached one hand in, summoning my flames. They sprang to life in my palm, illuminating the scene below.

The well wasn't as deep as I expected, only about twenty feet. Several roots had grown through here and there and there was even a small tree, broken downward by Anabel's fall. She lay at the bottom of the well, silent and unmoving. There was no sign of water, at least not now.

I reached in with both hands and summoned my strong winds. They howled in my ears as they tornadoed down the well, but they did as I wanted. They lifted Anabel up and carefully rose her toward the surface. Once she was out of the well, I took hold of her wrist, pulled her out from over the opening, and set her down. My winds lingered nearby, growling amid the grass.

"Anabel?" I checked her pulse.

To my relief, her heart still beat. I couldn't find any bleeding, though she remained unconscious. She was soaked through, despite me not having seen water in the well. And there was no sign of Liam's return. The shadow would have him running forever in that forest. It hadn't seemed exactly like a spirit, but it had to be the well's magic. A shade, perhaps—a collection of the people that it had claimed.

I brought my winds back and hovered them under her body, pulling her along by her wrists so it would look like I was dragging her if Liam returned. Soon enough, I had her in the back of the cruiser, wrapped up in my shawl. I turned up the vehicle's heat to the max.

Liam returned shortly after. "I lost them," he said as he jogged over. "I realized they were just leading m— You got her out?"

He stopped, his eyes widening in surprise as he saw Anabel shivering in his back seat.

"Yeah. I couldn't let her drown."

"If I'd known you got her out, I'd have kept chasing them. How did you get her out on your own?" Liam asked.

Oh, boy. How was I supposed to answer that? I searched for a reasonable answer, but nothing came to me. "It doesn't matter," I blurted. "Let's just get her—"

Anabel groaned.

Liam stepped around me to lean in closer to her. "Anabel?"

She squinted her eyes open. "What happened?"

"You were pushed into the well," Liam said softly. "Can you think of anyone who would do that?"

Anabel blinked several times and let out a shuddering breath. "Caleb."

Surprise rippled through me. "The mayor? Why? I know you two were fighting yesterday, but... why would he do that?"

"He's had a grudge against me since elementary school," Anabel said, straightening. "He was convinced I stole a baseball his grandfather gave him and made me the target of every smear campaign he could. I hate to admit it, but I retaliated in kind. He ran for class president, so did I. I made up vicious rumors, so did he."

Liam and I shared a glance. All this over a childhood grudge match?

Anabel caught the look and pulled my shawl tighter around herself. "I know it's pathetic. Every year it's seemed to grow more and more out of control. Especially this last year, when we were both running for mayor. I was so convinced that I had the vote of the people."

I rubbed the back of my neck. "I thought you did, too. You seemed to be more popular than Caleb. We all voted for you to be May Queen, after all."

"I accused him of stealing the vote," Anabel murmured. "I was ready to bring in the state police before I realized how stupid it all was. So, I made the decision. I was going to let this go. But Caleb didn't want to."

"Why not?" Liam asked. His voice was soft but probing.

Anabel winced. "Because I did steal his baseball when we were kids. I meant to give it back. I was just being a stupid kid. But I was playing with it here and... lost it in the well."

I turned to look at the old thing with its broken winch and old stones. It looked so innocuous. But was tonight really a culmination of everything that had happened since Anabel was an elementary school student?

Of course.

It was about the grudge. It was about the years and years of anger and hate that had built between them. The well hadn't latched onto the two of them because of their most recent fight, nor Anabel's wish on the street. It all went back to that baseball, the hostility between them when Anabel dropped it into the well.

"Why did you steal the baseball?" I pressed, playing on a hunch.

Liam gave me a slightly confused expression but didn't interrupt.

Anabel grimaced. "I had a crush on him. I was trying to get his attention."

Just as I thought. Owen Cook had been involved in a love affair gone wrong with Abigail. Howard Whitman had lied about Penelope Blackwood marrying him. It wasn't just random... I was willing to bet that if we looked at the other victims; they were tangled up in similar drama.

Which also meant I was wrong. Caleb was never the target of the magic. Anabel was the party that wronged him with the baseball, and the well would claim her, not him. I sighed as I leaned back, turning my face up to the sky. If I'd had more time, I might have been able to figure that out before now...

But it didn't matter. It was past midnight now, and I'd gotten Anabel out of the well. It meant that it was over. The well wouldn't still be coming after her, which meant I had another forty years before it tried to claim another victim.

"What do you think you're doing?" Liam asked sharply.

I turned back to find Anabel struggling weakly against the seatbelt he'd buckled around her.

"I'm fine," she insisted. "I have to get back to the well. If I can get the baseball out, then everything will be fine."

A chill ran down my spine. Maybe it was dawn, rather than midnight. I needed to worry about? Every forty years on May Day the well claimed someone. May Day had passed, hadn't it? She should be safe now!

Unless the corrupted magic was too strong. After four hundred years and ten victims, the well's reach could be growing. What if it could still get Anabel, even if she didn't die in the well itself?

I needed my books. I needed to look more into what all of this meant.

"Let's get back to town," I blurted, reaching around Liam to shut the door. She couldn't get out of the back of the cruiser, luckily. I grabbed Liam's arm. "I need to see the report on Owen Cook again."

He searched my face, but nodded.

We took Anabel to the hospital. She was growing more and more anxious, and the doctors ended up having to sedate her, as she was screaming that she needed to return to the well. Worry wrapped around my gut, but there wasn't anything we could do here.

We went to the B&B, where we sat in the living room and started to go through the file. It wasn't long before Abigail returned home, looking exhausted.

She frowned at us. "I didn't see either of you at the dance again. What's happening?"

I rubbed my bleary eyes. It'd been such a long day that I was exhausted! But there was still more work to be done. I had to figure out what was really going on.

"There's a pattern," I said. "In the victims. Anabel nearly died in the well tonight. Every forty years... there has to be something that links them."

Liam leaned back on the couch. "It's a coincidence, Harper. I'm sure that it's not only forty years apart, that's just a legend that people have made up. Unless you're saying that there is something magical happening."

"There's no such thing as magic," Abigail said immediately. Her voice was flat, rote, as though it was something she said all the time.

Yet I'd never heard her say anything like that before. I squinted at her, my suspicions rising. But there wasn't any time to think about that right now. Not when Anabel was still in danger. What was the key here? Why had Owen Cook been at the well? What drew Anabel back now?

The baseball.

The pieces clicked into place as I straightened. "We need to get everything out of the whispering well."

Liam rubbed his forehead. "Why?"

To break the curse! I cast about for an answer he'd accept. "Because I bet there's a lot more down there than anybody knows. And I think we'll find answers."

# 6

## BREAKING THE CURSE

Liam checked over the gear, yawning as he did so. I bounced on my toes, holding his coffee for him.

"Calm down," he told me. "Whatever is down there is going to keep long enough for me to make sure the harness isn't torn."

I winced. "Sorry. I guess this whole thing has me on edge. Is there anything I can do?"

"Make sure that the winch on the Jeep works properly."

I set the two coffees on the hood of the Jeep and checked the winch attached to the front of it. We'd be using this to lower Liam down into the well so he could check out what was down there. The hard hat he'd wear to protect him from falling rocks sat on the ground next to the ropes.

Ella and Max had volunteered to stay at the hospital with Anabel. They weren't the only ones, as Liam got police protection for her. He was still convinced that it'd been a person who tried to kill her. If I didn't know it was magic, I would have thought the same thing.

The active police were investigating what happened last night and were protecting Anabel now. The precinct captain didn't think the well had anything to do with it, though, so agreed that Liam and I could investigate it ourselves. He'd allowed Liam to sign out this equipment.

He even had his taser with him, though nobody—me included—thought it would be necessary to have.

"I still don't understand why you think this has anything to do with the attack on Anabel," Liam grumbled as he harnessed himself up.

"Because Anabel has been spearheading the drive to have the well restored. Maybe there's something in there connected to Owen Cook's death that someone didn't want found," I bluffed. "The well was never properly investigated. So maybe there's something left."

Liam gave me a searching glance. It was one that I'd grown to know too well. The one that made me think he knew I was lying and wanted to know what was really going on.

"I have a hunch," I added, hoping that would be enough to stop him from looking too deeply into it.

He returned to his work, and I stepped around him, reaching into my pocket. I didn't know how the well worked exactly and I wasn't sure it was safe for Liam to go in. He'd insisted and I couldn't argue with him to let me go in instead, though, so I had come up with another possibility.

I pulled a bracelet from my pocket. It'd been the last gift my parents had given me. I chewed my lip as I turned it over in my hands. If I was right, this would work. If I was wrong...

*I intend for Liam to be safe.* I tossed in the bracelet.

"What did you do that for?" Liam demanded.

I jumped as I turned. "You were busy! You weren't supposed to see."

Liam narrowed his eyes at me. "Harper, you're acting strange. Are you sure—"

"I'm sure. I just... was wishing for your safety," I admitted. Truthfully, I didn't think that the wish itself would make a difference. But giving it something so personal? I thought that would work. It would turn the well's magic from Liam onto me.

"I'm going to be fine," Liam promised me. He squeezed my hand lightly and stepped up to the well.

I went to the winch on the Jeep, opening it up slightly as Liam stepped over the wall. He lowered himself down into the well, the light from his headlamp soon disappearing. I stayed where I was, my hand on the winch so I could pull him out at a moment's notice.

Until a gunshot rang out. The bullet hit the Jeep, punching a hole into its hood.

I threw myself forward, rolling behind the well as gunshots continued firing. Liam shouted, his voice echoing in the well. My heart slammed against my throat as I crouched, searching the trees for who was firing at me. A shadowy figure melted among the branches, and then the glint of a rifle barrel aimed for me. I ducked again.

It was a person. A real person, not just a magic shade. What was going on here? Had it really been a living person who pushed Anabel into the well, rather than magic, as I'd thought?

"Harper!" Liam shouted as a lull came between gunshots. "My gear's jammed and I can't get up. I'm going to throw you the taser."

"Okay," I shouted back.

The taser arched out of the well's mouth. I lunged for it, but as it landed in my hands, another gunshot rang out. I was knocked to one side as pain flared in my arm. Clutching the taser, I dropped to the ground. Blood soaked through my sleeve, but I was in the midst of a bunch of overgrown weeds.

The shooter wouldn't be able to see if I'd been hit.

"Harper," Liam yelled. "Are you hit? Harper!"

I remained perfectly still and silent. Even with the taser, I had no chance against the shooter. Not unless they got closer.

The person crept from the trees and came toward me; the rifle clutched in their hands. I watched through slitted eyes, heart in my throat as I waited for the right moment.

From where I was lying, I couldn't see who the person was as they laid the rifle against the side of the well. I tightened my grip on the taser, turning it slightly. The shooter took a knife from their pocket and reached to cut Liam's rope.

"No!" I howled, making them jump and Liam shout.

I lifted the taser, aiming for the shooter. They lunged for me as I pressed the trigger. Two metal darts shot from the taser, hitting the shooter. They fell to the ground, shouting out in pain. I grabbed the rifle and threw it over my shoulder and then grabbed the knife.

Finally, I stopped the taser. The attacker lay on the ground, groaning. The voice was male, but he was masked, so I still didn't know who it was. Keeping an eye on him, I rushed around the well and activated the winch, raising Liam out of the well.

He took the taser from me and gestured for me to stay back as he approached the shooter. I held the knife tightly, though I wasn't sure what I'd do with it if the attacker sprang at Liam.

"You're under arrest for the attempted murder of Harper Nightshade," Liam said, turning the man onto his stomach. He quickly handcuffed the man and then dragged him to his feet.

Liam grabbed the back of the mask and yanked it off the man's head. I gasped, dropping the knife.

"Mayor Caleb?" I shouted in shock. "What are you... why... what?"

Caleb panted as he glared at me.

"Why were you shooting at us?" I demanded, marching over.

Liam recited the Miranda rights as I glowered at the mayor.

Caleb tried to shrug himself free of Liam, but couldn't loosen his grip. He glared at us both before he spat out, "You're going to pull everything out of that well anyway, aren't you? There's no point anymore. I stole the election! I made up a fake voting box I swapped after the polls closed. I tossed the original into the well so nobody would know."

I groaned, stepping back. "For real? All of this over that? And that's why you went after Anabel. Because if her restoration project went through, your duplicity would be revealed."

Liam hauled Caleb toward the Jeep. "That's pathetic, Mayor. And you'll have a long time behind bars to think about whether it was worth it."

# 7

# FACING TRUTHS

Liam set a box on the table, smiling softly at Abigail. "We recovered these from the well. They matched the descriptions of the items that Owen Cook stole from you forty years ago."

Abigail's eyes welled with tears as she pulled the box closer. I craned my neck to peer inside. Most of it was jewelry, but there was also a brass bell that drew my eye. It was perfectly intact, with no sign of tarnish on it despite being submerged in water for forty years. The magic of the well must have kept it from degrading.

"I've been studying the reports of his death, and I've reached the conclusion it was an accident," Liam continued, folding his hands over the table. "What I figure happened is that he was trying to get into the well to get the stuff he'd hidden, and ended up breaking his rope. He smashed his head on the way down and drowned."

"I never thought I'd see any of this again," Abigail murmured. She picked up a simple gold bracelet and smoothed her fingers over it. "Thank you, Detective Liam. This means more to me than you know."

He gave her a small nod.

"I just wish that Owen hadn't died. He was a charlatan and a cad, but he didn't deserve death like that." Abigail sighed as she put the bracelet back. "Am I free to keep these things, or does the precinct need to hold onto them for evidence?"

"They're yours to keep."

I rubbed Abigail's back as her eyes filled with tears. She carefully gathered the box in her arms.

"Thank you," she said again. "I'm going to need a few minutes."

"Of course," Liam agreed.

I sighed as Abigail left. Even though most mysteries had been solved now, there was still one weighing on my mind. Just how did Abigail know so much about what was going on in town? I suspected an answer, but I wasn't sure I wanted to dig into it.

Maybe I was worried about what I'd find. Maybe it was because I was reluctant to pry into Abigail's business. I wouldn't want anyone digging into me, after all. Everyone deserved their privacy. But I still felt like there was something more to learn here. Something important that I had to put to rest, one way or another.

"Harper, would you mind coming back to my place?" Liam asked.

My cheeks warmed as I turned to him. Why was he asking me to go back to his place?

"To talk. Privately," he added.

"We can talk here," I said.

Liam shook his head, his gaze strangely intense. "I need to talk to you with no interruptions."

My heart skipped a beat. I swallowed hard and nodded. My mind whirled as I considered everything he could want to talk to me about. My cheeks heated even more when he took my hand to lead me out of the B&B. I thought about telling Abigail I was heading out, but didn't want to interrupt her.

Liam was quiet on the way to his place. Once we were there, he gestured toward the kitchen. "Want some coffee?"

I nodded.

"We found a great deal in the well," he said as we headed into the kitchen. "Your bracelet, for one thing. Hundreds of coins, and a lot of even older things. The water was only a few inches deep, which is surprising considering how high the water table is right now."

He set his machine to make coffee and turned, giving me a piercing look. It was as though he was expecting me to offer an explanation.

"I guess we were lucky. Maybe the well is running dry," I suggested.

"That's a possibility," he agreed, his intense gaze unwavering.

"Did you find the baseball?" I asked quickly, hoping to distract him. I folded my arms, that feeling of guilt rising in me again. No matter how many times I told myself I had no reason to feel guilty, it never went away.

Liam broke eye contact to grab the coffee. He added some milk and handed it to me, then went about preparing his own coffee.

"We found the baseball," he said eventually. "Pristine, as though it'd been in there for hours rather than years. We also found a gold watch engraved with Howard Whitman's name. It was on the very bottom, buried beneath a couple of inches of mud. Which isn't a lot for four hundred years, is it?"

"I don't know, the well was covered for most of that time." I sipped my coffee absently.

With any luck, removing the items from the well, especially that watch, would have finally dispelled the curse on the well. It could go back to being a wishing well... that was, if the town restored it rather than simply burying it.

That wasn't up for me to decide. But I was sure that the well would no longer draw people to their deaths, at the very least.

"I'm glad that it worked out. And if you think about it, my wish came true." I smirked at Liam as he sat across from the table.

His brows pinched together. "What wish?"

"I wished that you'd be safe going into the well. And look at you now, safe and sound." I winked at him, but my mirth faded at the serious look on his face.

"What's wrong?" I asked, my voice low.

"There's something else, another reason I asked you here. There's something we need to discuss. About... well, us."

Liam stared down at his coffee. He twitched on the spot, his nerves growing more apparent. My heart beat faster. I'd never seen him nervous like this before. Without warning, the details of the last three months grew stronger in my mind.

We'd spent so much time together. We'd grown close, and that closeness grew more pronounced every day.

I hadn't just wished for him to be safe in the well because I cared about him as a friend. I'd have done the same for anyone, but for Liam, there was something extra. I didn't want to admit my growing feelings, too afraid that it would ruin everything that we'd been building...

Was it possible I wasn't the only one with feelings?

"Ever since the Winter Festival, strange things have been happening here in Moonhaven," he said slowly.

The heat in my cheeks turned cold.

"I don't like it. Not one bit. I like even less that I have no answers what is going on." He sipped his coffee and looked up, skewering me with his gaze. "I know that there has to be a logical explanation, but I can't see what it is."

I opened my mouth to ask him what strange things he was talking about, but couldn't. I couldn't even look away from him. A prickle ran across the back of my neck.

"The only thing I can see clearly in all of this is that its directly related to you," Liam said.

*Come on, say something!* I finally tore my gaze away and focused on my mug. "I don't know what you mean. I know there's a lot of weird things happening, but they have nothing to do with me."

"Don't they?"

I looked up, leveling my chin at him. "Are you saying that I'm some sort of mastermind going around killing people?"

"Only one person in town has died since you came into town."

"Then what are you saying?"

Liam stood. He strode to the drawer next to the sink and opened it. "I'm saying that I made a wish, too. To find something I lost, remember? I lost it when I got that blow to the head. It wasn't where I'd put it before, and I couldn't remember what I did with it. But my wish was granted—I found it now."

He came back and slid a notebook across the table to me.

My hands shook as I opened it. Liam's neat writing crowded the pages. My stomach swooped as I read the meticulous notes he'd made about me. How I acted with the Winter Festival, then at Valentine's

Day, and even a great deal with what happened at the Spring Equinox.

I felt frozen all the way through as I looked up at him. His eyes were hard as rocks as he leaned forward in full police mode.

"You need to tell me what's going on," he said. "And don't leave anything out."

The End

Did you enjoy *May Fay Murmurs*?

Please consider rating it on Amazon, Goodreads, or Bookbub.

Reviews help me reach new readers.

Read ***Midsummer Mischief***, the next story in the ***Mystic Moonhaven Mysteries***.

Have you read the *Jane and Kennedy Daniels Mysteries*, the *Annie Archer Paranormal Mysteries*, the *Wilma Wade Holiday Mysteries*, the *Mike and Maddie Mysteries,* or the *Pine Grove Mysteries*?

# 1

## SOLSTICE SHADOWS

Ella, my best friend, eyed my drumming fingers as she stopped by the table I occupied all by myself in her coffee shop. "Harper, I think you've had enough coffee. Why not switch to decaf?"

I forced my hand to lie flat, then heaved a sigh. "Coffee has nothing to do with it."

Ella's eyes widened as she glanced around. Ella's Wheel was packed today. She leaned in close and lowered her voice. "Is it magic or Liam?" she asked.

Normally, I would find her questions endearing. They reminded me that someone in this town cares about me despite being a relatively recent addition. I'd only lived in Moonhaven for about eighteen months now. While I had a solid group of friends, I was still the whacky newcomer with the weird occult bookstore. Thankfully, I'd recently moved into the small studio over the store I'd been working on for the past three months. The less people knew about my private life, the better.

"It's not Liam," I grumbled. The lie was obvious even to me.

Detective Liam Ashford was one of those friends I had in Moonhaven. At least he was. I wasn't sure where we stood in our relationship anymore. Not since he revealed he had been keeping meticulous notes on me with the mysterious happenings in town. It was like a slap in the face... or a threat.

I shook those thoughts off. "Something is off about the magical energy here in town," I whispered so nobody else could hear me. "It's just like the other times. I think something is going to happen."

Ella's brows pinched together in worry. "You need to talk to Liam about it."

"I can't."

Ella sucked on her teeth and then pointed toward the door that led into the back. "Go upstairs. I'll be up in a minute to talk."

I almost protested—I had to get back to my bookstore. But business had been lackluster for the last month. People were more interested in getting outdoors and in the sun than they were in reading. So I shrugged and headed into the back, where I waved at the baker and trudged upstairs. Her upstairs apartment was decorated in shades of blue and green, creating a soothing underwater vista.

Ella joined me shortly. She put her honey-brown hair up into a bun and plopped onto the couch next to me. I grabbed a seashell-shaped pillow and hugged it to my chest, lowering my chin as I stared at the floor.

"What's going on? You two have been on the outs for weeks," Ella said. "And I don't get it."

My nose wrinkled. "After what happened during the May Day festival, Liam showed me a notebook he'd been keeping. He's been studying me, taking notes, connecting me to everything that's been happening. It's like he thinks I'm responsible."

"Did you tell him the truth?"

I shook my head. "I can't tell him about magic. I shouldn't even have told you and Max. The only reason I did was because I had no other choice."

Ella's brow furrowed. "Max is a witch, too, though."

"Doesn't matter. He'll tell you the same thing. We're not supposed to tell anyone."

"Alright." She looked unconvinced but, to her credit, didn't push. "What can I do to help, then?"

"Keep an eye out and let me know if you or anyone else notices anything strange that happens around town."

"I can do that. I am, after all, manager of the Moonhaven Rumor Mill," she said, then laughed.

Ella loved gossip, and everyone knew she did. She'd never spread things that could actually hurt people, though. It was one reason I loved her so much.

We headed back downstairs, finding the shop a little emptier than it had been when Ella took her break. My table had been taken by Abigail, my former landlady who ran the B&B across the street... and Liam. I hesitated. I wanted to talk to Abigail, but I could do that later, right?

On the other hand, I shouldn't let Liam drive me away from the things I liked.

I headed over. "Hi, Abigail."

"Harper." She smiled at me. "I saw your store was closed for lunch and thought you might be here."

Liam looked distinctively unhappy to see me. He stared down at the coffee in his hands, his usually calm and relaxed demeanor tense.

"Well, I'm headed back to the store now," I told Abigail. "If you want to stop by to chat, I'd love to."

I headed for the door. A chair scraped against the floor behind me and a prickly sensation washed over the back of my neck, but I didn't stop. Liam caught up with me on the sidewalk.

"Harper, wait," he called.

I slowed down and glanced back at him. "What?"

"I just want to ask how you're doing," he said.

I turned back to him, folding my arms. He was a handsome man and the puppy-dog eyes he was giving me right now made me falter. I took a deep breath and reminded myself of what he did. "You watch me so closely. You should already know how I'm doing."

I tightened my arms around myself. I was supposed to be his friend, not a suspect. Why should I be the first to apologize when he hadn't apologized to me?

Liam opened his mouth, and I found I didn't even want to hear an apology. That really was unfair of me, I know, but I was still angry. I turned on my heel and walked away without waiting to hear what he had to say.

I almost hoped he'd follow. But he didn't.

I got back to my store and flung open the door, stomping inside, only to stop dead when I saw it wasn't empty. A woman sat in the middle of the floor, rocking back and forth in a rocking chair that hadn't been there a moment ago. Her hair was the same shade of gray as Abigail's, with big brown eyes. She wore clothes that reminded me of the early sixteen hundreds.

I swallowed hard as I met the woman's eyes. She had a slightly transparent quality to her and the rocking chair made no noise against the hardwood floor.

"What are you doing here?" I asked as I closed the door behind me.

"I never found out what happened to my daughter, and the veil has been mighty thin between Moonhaven and the other side this year," the woman replied. She sounded as though she could have stepped in from outside, rather than coming from another century. "The name's Gail Blackwood."

My eyes widened. "Penelope's mother?"

She nodded once.

I studied her. Her large eyes were hard and wary, as though she had had a very hard life. There was something familiar about them, though. I automatically thought of David Blackwood, the museum curator. But before I could study his face in my memory, another one arrived in my mind. Abigail Thorne.

"Is your full name Abigail, by any chance?" I asked.

"Yes. I go by Gail, though." Gail rocked harder. "If you can help me find my daughter, let me know. Otherwise, stay out of my way."

She disappeared with a chill wind.

I shivered, despite the heat of midsummer. Outside, everything was in bloom, but the interior of my shop was cold now, even though my AC didn't work that great. I hesitated a moment before I closed my eyes and opened my palms. I sent out my searching winds, and they came back with the distinctive feeling of a spirit's lingering presence.

I'd had some false positives in the past, but this time I was certain.

Gail Blackwood's spirit had come to Moonhaven. Was it just a coincidence that she shared the same name as the B&B owner?

This gave me something to focus on, though. The uneasy energy I'd been feeling around town lately could very well be related to Gail.

I headed back to Ella's Wheel. Abigail was still there talking with Liam, and I hesitated. It could wait. I didn't have anything that needed to be resolved right at this exact second. I didn't need to face off with Liam again.

On the other hand, why should I let him control what I did? If he wanted to take notes on my actions, he could. It wasn't as though he was going to figure out I was talking to ghosts just because I asked Abigail a few questions.

I stepped inside and headed over to their table. "Abigail, I forgot I wanted to ask you something. I've been looking into the Penelope Blackwood thing again lately, and I learned that her mother's name was Gail. Do you have any family history in Moonhaven?"

"If there is, I'm not aware of it," Abigail said, raising her eyebrows toward her hairline. She frowned at me, as though she wasn't happy that I'd even asked. "My father moved us to Moonhaven when I was young."

There was a slightly sharp note to her voice. Was she being cagey or was she chastising me for interrupting her conversation with Liam?

"Why do you ask?" Liam asked me.

I wrinkled my nose. "I'm just curious. Abigail, I'm going to close up shop for the rest of the day. I'm going to the museum to catch up with David, and I'll stop by the B&B later to chat. Okay?"

"Yes, that's fine," Abigail said.

Liam shot me a frustrated look. I ignored it as I turned away once more. He had my number. He could text me an apology at the very least. It didn't have to be this big scene, nor did he have to be alone with me to apologize. Maybe he was frustrated, but he only had himself to blame for taking notes on me as though I was a criminal.

If I was completely honest with myself, though, I'd admit that it wasn't just an apology that I was looking for. When he gave me that notebook and I asked him why he did that, he hadn't answered. Only told me I needed to tell him everything.

As though I could! I wanted to tell him. I wanted to share all the strange things, the connections between them, and the way I kept digging up more and more about Moonhaven's past. It killed me to have to keep everything hidden away like this.

But I had to. I couldn't tell him.

Tell no one. That was a witch's creed. And I'd broken it out of necessity with Ella, when a spell was killing her. Liam didn't need to know. He couldn't know. I could never tell him anything.

And so how was this gulf between us ever supposed to close?

## 2

# ENCHANTED EVENING

Moonhaven didn't have any official celebrations for the midsummer solstice, but that didn't mean that there weren't private celebrations.

Anabel Marley, our new mayor whom Liam and I had rescued from the old mayor during the events of May Day —long story— welcomed me into her home that evening. She was dressed in a gown with layers of different shades of green, with a delicate tiara made to look like flowers and branches perched on her head. She beamed at me as she hugged me.

"I'm so glad you made it, Harper," Anabel gushed. "Come on in. The party's getting started. We have board games in the dining room, dancing in the living room, and, of course, plenty of coffee, energy drinks, and other things to keep us awake through the shortest night of the year!"

"Always glad to party," I replied with a laugh.

Everyone was dressed in the 'fantasy woodland' theme that Anabel had decorated her house with. There were a few people, who, like Anabel, dressed like a forest nymph. Most people stuck various types of ears on their heads. Some people were more like Peter Pan or Robin Hood.

I'd worn a green shirt and brown pants. Not very woodland now that I saw the lengths other people went to, but at least I matched the general décor.

I wandered into the living room, where there was less dancing and more standing around the edges of the room, listening to music and chatting. As I looked around, I saw David Blackwood. We'd talked earlier at the museum and I was about to see if Ella had arrived yet when I realized who David was talking to... Liam.

They seemed engrossed in their conversation as I made a beeline for them. What could they be talking about? Liam didn't seem to be interested in Moonhaven's history. Was he checking up on me because I said I was going to visit the museum earlier?

"What are you two talking about?" I asked when I arrived next to them.

David jumped, as though he hadn't realized I was there. Liam sipped at whatever he was drinking, his blue eyes not leaving David's face. He gave no indication I was even there.

"Liam was just seeing if I'd found more information on Penelope Blackwood for you," David explained. "I was telling him that so far there's nothing to indicate she ever returned to Moonhaven."

My shoulders tensed. What was Liam checking up on me like this for? I had hoped, in the few seconds it took me to get over here, that I was just being paranoid. Yet it seemed like it was, in fact, a valid concern.

I struggled to keep my expression smooth. "I hardly expected you to find anything after just a few hours."

David laughed. "True, but I've found a few promising leads. I've actually been looking more into the Blackwood family tree since January. I've found quite a bit of interesting things concerning her genealogy. I'll have a package for you tomorrow about everything."

"Thanks." I wasn't sure how genealogy would help me find out what exactly happened to Penelope Blackwood, but it was something.

Four hundred years ago, Howard Whitman had used magic to make Penelope disappear, then claimed that they had been married so he could inherit all the lands that belonged to her. I thought it was pretty likely that she had been killed, but maybe there was a way to find her bones and bring Gail some peace... and if Gail, being on the other side, didn't know what happened to her daughter then maybe Penelope was still lingering around here on the mortal plane somewhere.

In any case, I could help. So long as Liam didn't mess things up.

"Do you mind if I talk with Detective Ashford for a moment alone?" I asked David.

He moved off, and I pulled Liam closer to the corner before I turned on him. "What do you think you're doing?"

"You're acting strange again." His usually expressive eyes were blank.

I folded my arms. "Strange?"

"The last few days you've been twitchy and short-tempered," he said, mirroring me. "You've been looking into the history of the town again, and you only do that when something weird is about to happen. You're acting the same way you did before everything else that happened."

I inhaled sharply through my nose. Even when I wasn't talking to him, he could see what was happening to me. I wanted to say that I hated it, but I had to admit that I was more than a little... I don't know, maybe flattered? I wasn't sure how I was supposed to react to my own feelings.

"I'm not acting strange at all. I'm just mad at you," I told him.

He dropped his arms and reached out, taking my hand lightly. His fingers wrapped around mine as the mask dropped from his face.

Regret was written so deeply in his eyes that it took my breath away.

"I know I scared you with that notebook," he murmured. "And I'm sorry. I didn't mean to. I just want to know the truth about what's happening in Moonhaven. Can't you tell me that?"

The earnestness in his gaze left me wavering. As upset as I still was with him about this whole thing, I missed having him around. I'd gotten used to our morning walks, watching TV together, just hanging out. I hated we had so much of a gulf between us. I didn't want things to get worse.

But he just said exactly why I couldn't fix things. He wanted the truth, which was the one thing that I couldn't offer him.

I turned my face away to hide my emotions, only to stiffen and gasp. There, in the middle of the dancefloor, was Gail Blackwood. Her gaze was laser-focused on a young woman I vaguely recognized. Her name was Chloe, I thought—she came into my store every so often looking for new romances. She was dancing with a young man.

Before I could go over, though, the music cut out. Anabel stood next to the speakers, and she clapped her hands. "Twilight is officially over. It's now the night! Let's all step outside for some fireworks."

Gail disappeared. I started forward, hoping to get to Chloe as everyone streamed from the house. But even as I did so, Liam tugged on my hand. He hadn't let go, and I hadn't pulled away. I bit my lip as I turned back toward him.

"What's happening?" he demanded.

I stared into his dark blue eyes, and the truth lingered on the tip of my tongue. It would be so easy to tell him everything... but then I thought about how he'd look at me if I did tell him everything. He might realize that strange things were happening in Moonhaven, but he had no idea it was on the mystical side of things.

If there was one thing Liam Ashford didn't believe in, it was magic. A bitter laugh caught in my throat. Even if I dared to tell him...

"I can't tell you, and if I did, you wouldn't believe me."

He dropped my hand. "Can't or won't? It makes a difference."

"It does," I agreed. "Which is why when I say I can't tell you, I mean it."

Liam growled softly as he dragged his hand through his hair. The sound startled me; I hadn't realized he was this frustrated! But then, I had been evading him for some time. It was likely that he was just as frustrated as I was by this entire business.

The booming of the fireworks started outside. We both paused, glancing at the window. A burst of light lit the backyard, but none of the fireworks could be seen from this angle. I thought about trying to get back outside, but right now I didn't even want to look at the light show.

"Why?" Liam demanded. "Why can't you tell me?"

"Because of reasons that I can't tell you."

He groaned as he rubbed his hands over his face. "So then I guess

I'll just have to keep looking on my own, huh? I'll have to figure out what you're hiding from me."

I closed my eyes, fighting back the urge to snap at him. This wasn't a threat. He was merely stating a fact. Knowing Liam, it was torture for him to have so much that he didn't understand. Could I really blame him for that?

"If you trust me, then you won't," I told him.

"How can I trust you when you're keeping secrets from me?"

"You keep secrets from me, too. You don't tell me everything about the cases you work on."

"That's not the same!" Liam threw his hands into the air. "Those are details I can't tell you. You know that."

I nodded, my heart beating shallowly. This reminded me too much of the fight we'd had when he first showed me his notebook. I hated it. I didn't want to fight with Liam. I wanted this to blow over as though it had never happened in the first place.

"You can't tell me," I agreed. "Which is why it's exactly the same."

Liam searched my face, understanding dawning on his face. Confusion followed quickly. Would it be enough for him to stop asking questions when I couldn't give him answers? Or would it just make him ask even more questions?

"We should go outside," I murmured, my shoulders slumping. "It sounds like the fireworks are already over."

Anabel appeared in the doorway. "There you two are! Have you seen Chloe?"

"Not since everyone went outside," I answered. The worry on Anabel's face sent a chill down my spine. "What happened?"

"I'm sure she's around somewhere. Her boyfriend noticed she was missing and we haven't been able to find her. Her car is still here, though... I don't know where she would have gone to. Maybe she took a walk or something. Or maybe someone drove her home..."

"We'll come look," Liam said, striding forward.

We headed outside. People were calling for Chloe and more than one person grumbled about the party being ruined. I headed to look through the parked cars, thinking maybe she'd taken a breather. There were no answers to my calls, though.

When I got to her car, I caught sight of a fluttering white thing tucked into the handle of the car. I plucked it out, finding a carefully embroidered handkerchief.

My heart sank. The corner had an elaborate 'GB' on it. Gail Blackwood.

Oh, no. Had Chloe been kidnapped by a ghost?

# 3

# NIGHT OF REVELATIONS

"What do you have there?"

I jumped, whirling. Liam stood a little way down from me, craning his neck toward the handkerchief as he approached. I held it out to him silently. When he took it, his brow furrowed. He turned it over in his hands and looked back up at me.

"I found it in her door handle," I explained.

Liam's expression tightened. "Nobody saw her leave, and I have a funny feeling about all of this. Will you help me find her?"

I twisted my hands together, searching his face in the darkness. The last vestiges of twilight had disappeared, and the night was only broken by a crescent moon hanging above us in the sky. My heart twinged; he was offering an olive branch here, and I wasn't sure if I could take it.

Did this mean he'd accepted that I had things he couldn't know? Or was it—

Gail Blackwood appeared at my elbow, making me jump. She looked around, her expression morphing from confusion to irritation. She turned to me and glanced me up and down. "I wondered what I was hearing. It's you again. I've seen a bunch of your conversations with this man. If you can't trust him, why are you spending so much time with him?"

The air left my lungs, her words as powerful as a punch to the stomach. The warnings my parents drilled into me flooded my mind, but that still rang in my ears.

Did I trust Liam? I'd spent the last six or more months wanting to tell him the truth. But my parents found each other and told one another that they were witches. How could I go through my life constantly hiding that vital part of me?

"What is it?" Liam asked, looking right through Gail.

I opened my mouth to tell him nothing. To continue the lie... but when he looked back at me and our eyes met, I couldn't. I didn't want to keep these secrets from him. I didn't want to keep lying and being frustrated and angry. I didn't want to be the one that made it so this gulf between us couldn't be bridged.

He shared those notes with me for a reason. He wasn't accusing me of anything. It was a plea, an offering.

"You're not going to like it," I said slowly. "And you probably won't believe me."

His brow furrowed.

I sighed as I leaned against the side of Chloe's car. "Ever since I was a child, the one rule that's been drilled into me over and over is never to tell anyone. Let no one know. It's..."

"I thought you said you couldn't tell me," Liam said. His voice was flat.

"I shouldn't, the same way you shouldn't tell anyone about your cases, but technically it's possible." I took a deep breath, preparing to say the words out loud. Why did they feel so heavy on my tongue? "I'm a witch. Everything that's been happening in Moonhaven is magic.

"First it started with the Winter Festival. Percival Whitman used magic to attack David Blackwood. The unnatural frost, the wolves people were seeing? It was all magic. All him. On Valentine's Day, I used magic to figure out the secret messages in those letters."

I paused to get a read on him, but in the darkness, I couldn't see his face clearly. Was any of this having an impact? I plunged on. "On the

Spring Equinox, a collection of curses were weighing down on Ella, because she's a descendant of all the original founders of Moonhaven. Four hundred years' worth of generational curses were going to kill her. The disappearances of artifacts from the museum were related to magic."

"And is magic the reason for my memory loss?" Liam asked. His voice was low and still emotionless. My heart sank somewhere down to my toes. He didn't believe me.

"In a way," I admitted. "You were helping me remove the spell from her when the bell crashed through the ceiling. Magically, that is. It struck your head, and that's what made you forget."

Gail grunted as she folded her arms. "Are you done yet?"

I sighed and gestured to her. "And I'm distracted because Gail Blackwood is standing right here. Her ghost, that is, and I'm suspecting that she has something to do with Chloe's disappearance."

"A ghost?" Liam repeated, the disbelief clear in his voice.

"Why, I never!" Gail glared at me. Unlike Liam, her features were perfectly visible. Her nostrils flared as she shook her finger at me. "I thought you might be useful in looking for my Penelope, but I can see I was mistaken."

"A ghost kidnapped Chloe?" Liam asked again.

I shook my head. "She's saying that she didn't. She wants to find out what happened to Penelope."

Liam shook his head and turned away.

Gail pinched her lips tightly together. "All I want to know is what happened to her. All these years, terrified for her. I haven't even gone to the other side properly, because I just know her spirit is lost. And then you accuse me of doing the same to some other girl's mother?"

"That's not what I meant," I said.

"That's exactly what you said," Gail replied. She continued to glare at me, then vanished.

Liam rubbed his temples. "I don't understand what you're talking about, Harper. How can any of that be true?"

I winced at his words, my stomach swooping. "I told you, you wouldn't believe it."

"Harper—"

"Hey, what are you—" someone came running up next to Liam, only to stop. The flashlight on a cell phone flashed into our faces. I shielded my eyes. "Oh, Detective Ashford. What are you doing here?"

I stepped to one side so the beam of light wasn't blinding me. A young man, the one Chloe had been dancing with, stood a little ways away, along with Anabel, a redheaded woman, and a couple other people I didn't know.

"We were looking for Chloe," Liam replied, his voice smooth. "Any sign of her?"

"Nah, not yet," the man said. He looked over at me. "Aren't you Harper Nightshade?"

I extended my hand. "Sure am. Liam asked me to help him out a bit."

"Trevor. I'm Chloe's boyfriend. And this here is Angelica," he added, gesturing toward the redheaded woman.

"I'm Chloe's best friend," she said, sounding oddly defensive. "She's not in her car, is she? I told her not to go wandering around at night. During the fireworks, she started talking about walking home."

Trevor sighed. "I wouldn't worry too much. She has a habit of running off like this."

Anabel gestured us all back to the house. "Let's get back to the party, shall we? Trevor and Angelica are right. I've known Chloe for a few years. She does like to go off and do her own thing."

Liam and I shared a glance. He tucked the handkerchief into his pocket as we headed back toward the house. We both lingered behind the group, but unfortunately, we would not have any time to talk about what I'd just told him. Trevor stayed back with us.

"Detective, if I'm honest, I think Chloe might have skipped town," he murmured to Liam. "She owes our landlord almost a full year's rent. She's been talking for months about just running off and disappearing. I don't know, but it might be good to have people on the lookout for her in other cities."

"I'll take that into advisement," Liam replied. "But if she was walking back to her home, we'll wait to see if she's even left first."

I frowned at him, but he caught my hand in the darkness as I opened my mouth. He squeezed my fingers, as though telling me to be quiet. I shut my mouth again. I wasn't sure what was going on here, and what any of it had to do with Gail. It must have a connection somewhere, but what was it?

Back at the house, Trevor headed off into the kitchen. Liam leaned close to my ear.

"I'm going to talk with the boyfriend more. You go see what Anabel thinks of Chloe, if this is like her or not," he murmured.

The feeling of his breath against my ear sent shivers down my spine. My heartbeat increased, although there was another reason for that—excitement that maybe Liam did trust me after all. He clearly thought more was happening here than we were being told.

I went off in search of Anabel, finding her in one of the upstairs rooms, where a rather impressive-looking Dungeons and Dragons game was being played.

"Hey, can we talk a bit?" I asked her.

"Sure."

We stepped into the hallway, and Anabel gave me a grin. "What's up?"

"Well..." I shrugged and laughed softly, as though embarrassed. "Honestly, I'm still a little worried about Chloe. Her boyfriend said that she's got some debt issues and may have skipped town."

Anabel leaned against the wall. "Honestly? It wouldn't surprise me. Chloe and I have been friends for a while, but things have been strained between us. I invested in a business venture she proposed, but it fell apart before she could get a start. Chloe is very avoidant of conflict."

"So you think she skipped town?"

"I think she probably got a bit too tipsy and left." Anabel shrugged. "Chloe doesn't like parties. Trevor's the one who insisted she come along. Although..."

"Although what?"

"It's probably nothing," Anabel said, though her expression said otherwise. "It's just that I've noticed a few things between Trevor and

Angelica. Small touches, lingering glances. It's probably harmless, but I just get this gut feeling... Oh, but I shouldn't gossip like this."

She shook her head while I turned over what she had just said. If Chloe's boyfriend and best friend had something going on, maybe she found out about it? That would explain her sudden departure... If that was the case, then maybe she really did just go home, and they were too embarrassed to admit it.

"What about you and the detective?" Anabel asked.

My head jerked up. "What about us?"

She gave me a knowing smile. "I've noticed how the two of you interact, too. So where are you at in your relationship?"

"We're not—" My cheeks turned hot as I spluttered. "There's no relationship."

Her knowing smile increased. "You should be open with him, Harper. He feels the same way. You're only holding yourself back."

I ducked my head. "Er, I have to go."

"I'm sorry if I overstepped," Anabel said.

"I have to go," I repeated.

I hurried back down the stairs, though I couldn't miss the tinkling laugh from Anabel. Honestly! What was that question even about? I smoothed down my shirt as I wove between the partygoers. I spied Liam with Trevor in the kitchen and slipped in, though I ignored them and went to the coffee machine.

"Chloe and I have been having a rough patch," Trevor admitted to Liam. "I was thinking she might step out on me."

"Ahh. And you two decided to be exclusive?" Liam asked.

Trevor shrugged. "We hadn't really talked it through, but yeah, that was where I thought it was."

"So you've been exclusive to her?"

"Whoa." Trevor frowned at him. "I'm not sure any of this is your business."

Liam lifted his hands. "Sorry. I've been drinking a bit and I guess my filter's gone. You're right, it's none of my business. But since she texted you, I suppose there's nothing to be worried about. Harper! I didn't see you."

I jumped and turned with a fresh cup of coffee. Liam grinned at me as he brushed past Trevor to grab my hand. "Ella called. She wants us to stop by. You ready to go?"

I set the coffee down and let him pull me away. As we passed through the doorway, I glanced back at Trevor, who watched us with narrowed eyes. And right beside him was Gail Blackwood.

## 4

# SECRETS UNDER THE STARS

At Ella's Wheel, I told Liam what Anabel had told me. The coffee shop was empty except for Ella, who we quickly brought up to speed with what was happening. Liam explained that Trevor and Angelica both seemed somewhat rattled, and he wasn't sure that he believed their excuses.

"Don't you have to wait twenty-four hours before you investigate?" Ella asked, resting her elbows on the table.

Liam shook his head. "That's movie nonsense. The first twenty-four hours are crucial to finding the missing person. Although I suppose if magic is involved, there isn't much we can do about it."

I stiffened at his sarcastic tone, but Ella's jaw dropped.

"I thought you couldn't tell him," she said, whirling on me. "Didn't you say that you're not supposed to tell anyone?"

Liam tensed. He narrowed his eyes, not at Ella but at me. "So, you're not supposed to tell anyone, but you told Ella?"

"She was under a spell. I told you that," I said, my hands clenched. "And just because you don't believe me doesn't mean it's not true."

"I never said I don't believe you."

Ella glanced between us, her eyes wide and expression regretful.

A muttered swear behind me made me jump. I turned, heart

hammering, but sagged in relief when I saw it was only Gail. We hadn't just accidentally revealed my magic to yet another person here in Moonhaven. I rubbed my temples.

"Gail Blackwood is back," I said.

"Back?" Ella repeated.

Gail passed through her and sank into the booth. "Why, when I'm trying to look for my daughter, do I keep getting pulled back to you?"

"Hold on a minute," I told her, then turned to Liam and Ella. "This is going to get confusing, listening to one half of the conversation." I leaned over the table toward Gail. "You told me earlier that you haven't gone to the other side. Why not?"

"Because I have to find my daughter."

"But can't you come back over every so often?" I pressed. "The veil is thin around Moonhaven. Can't you peek through?"

Gail shook her head. "It doesn't work like that. At least not for me. I'm stuck in a halfway point, not really here and not really there. Not until I can find my Penelope. I have spent the last four hundred years performing the searching ritual every midsummer."

I rubbed the back of my neck. "Even if you are right and she survived Howard Whitman's attack, it has been four hundred years. Penelope will have died by this time, by old age, if nothing else."

"Yes, she will have. And yet, I haven't even been able to find her bones." Gail groaned as she passed her hand over her eyes. "I can't move on until I know what happened to her. It's the only way I'll find her spirit to bring it home."

I nodded slowly. "So, you've been brought back to Moonhaven every midsummer?"

"My magic is tied closely to the sun and its seasons. But this is the first time anyone in town has seen me or interacted with me," Gail said.

Ella touched my hand. "Catch us up?"

I nodded and explained everything. Liam's expression was hard and blank, like he wasn't sure if he believed any of it. It was about what I expected from him, so I tried my best to ignore the knot growing in the pit of my stomach.

"If Gail has a searching spell, we can use it to find Chloe," Ella said, her eyes bright.

I turned to Gail hopefully.

She folded her arms, a dark expression on her face. "Oh, I can share my spell with you... but you have to do something for me first."

"What? But you said you didn't want another mother to go through—"

"I said I wouldn't put another mother through what I'd been through," Gail corrected. "But I also heard enough at that... party to know that this Chloe girl isn't right in the head. She probably ran off like that boy suggested. So. You find out what happened to Penelope and I'll give you the spell."

I fisted my hands together. "Chloe's life could be in danger. I promise I'll look for Penelope, but you need to give us the spell first!"

Gail gave me a hard grin. "No. I really don't."

She disappeared, giving herself the last word. I groaned as I threw myself back against my seat, covering my face.

"What happened?" Ella asked.

"She will not help unless we find out what happened to Penelope Blackwood," I groaned. I lowered my hands again, frowning. "Abigail seemed to be cagey when I brought it up to her... maybe she knows more than she's letting on. Maybe we should look into—"

Liam grunted. "You mean look into her to find out what she knows when she has nothing to do with this case?"

I stared at him, confused at the hostile tone.

"That's exactly what I did with you... that you got angry at me for doing," he said, leaning forward.

Ella cleared her throat. "I think I should go... call David Blackwood and see if we can get into the museum."

I opened my mouth to protest—or beg her to stay here with me—but she scurried away too quickly. Which was just as well. I sighed heavily as I leaned my elbows on the table. It would be best for Liam and I to have an actual talk. We'd been interrupted before.

"So. If you're a witch, why couldn't you tell me about it?" Liam asked brusquely. "Beyond not thinking I'd believe you, I mean."

I traced the grains of wood on the table with a finger. "It's the number one rule for all witches. Tell no one. I wanted to tell you. If I hadn't been terrified for Ella's safety, I would have been relieved when you learned about it during the equinox. Only... then you hit your head."

"But why do you have to keep it a secret?"

"You know the history of witch hunts. You know how many people were killed for being witches," I said slowly, then lifted my gaze to his. He stared at me intently. "There are still witch hunters out there. They might not be officially sanctioned like they used to be, but they're there. And they still kill witches."

A furrow appeared between his eyes. "How? If people are running around burning other people at the stake—"

"You're a detective. How many people are murdered or go missing in a year? How many unsolved cases are there?" I demanded.

Liam was quiet for a long moment before he slowly nodded. "Alright. So you couldn't tell me because you were afraid for your safety. When I showed you those notes I was keeping on you... you were afraid it'd bring these witch hunters down on you?"

"It meant I wasn't being careful enough."

"Then maybe it's something you should consider with Abigail. If she's keeping secrets from you, maybe she has valid reasons, too. Besides, I don't see how she could have anything to do with any of this. She wasn't at the party, and as for Gail Blackwood, what could Abigail have to do with a ghost?"

"I... they have the same first name," I said weakly.

Liam gave me a look that clearly told me it wasn't good enough. "Lots of people are named Abigail. That doesn't mean they have anything to do with a specific Abigail that lived four hundred years ago."

He was right, of course. I had no reason to think that Abigail was connected to any of this, other than the vaguest notion that somehow she was a descendant of Gail. And really, was it at all likely that was the case? It didn't matter, either, not unless Abigail being alive somehow proved that Penelope had survived Howard Whitman.

Was I just using this as a reason to put more distance between Liam and me? I didn't know.

Liam cleared his throat. "We should focus on the case at hand. If you believe a ghost can help us find Chloe, then you should investigate how you see fit. I, for one, am going to follow the money. Angelica claims Chloe scammed Anabel. I got a copy of her finances while we were searching. She's been taking out five thousand dollars a month, cash."

"How did you get a copy of her finances so quickly?" I asked, stunned.

"I made a few calls while you were talking with Anabel." Liam leaned forward again. "I think Chloe was being blackmailed. And I think that it's related to her disappearance tonight. Money usually reveals the truth of what's happening in these places."

I folded my arms. "You mean like how it revealed Percival Whitman was using magic to attack people in January?"

He grinned at me. "It revealed Percival Whitman had reason to attack David Blackwood since David found proof that the Whitmans didn't own as much land as they claimed."

"Oh. Oh... that... actually makes a lot of sense," I said, stunned.

Liam nodded. "I'm going to track down where the money went."

"And I'm going to find out what happened to Penelope Blackwood, so I can get a searching spell," I replied. "My searching winds don't have enough range for me to run around looking for Chloe myself."

"Searching winds?"

I grinned at him and lifted my hands. "One of my proficiencies is with wind. I have different types. Ones that lift, ones that search, ones that warm, others that chill. I used my lifting winds to pull Anabel Marley out of the whispering well in May."

Liam grunted, looking somewhere between unconvinced and impressed. "Alright. Let me know what you find."

## 5

# THE SOLSTICE SPELL

The darkness pressed against the museum windows like a living thing. I stifled a yawn as the coffee pot finished percolating. I'd gotten the key from David Blackwood, but I was here at the museum all by myself. I couldn't help but feel a little creeped out, especially considering that it was here at the museum that Percival Whitman's frost wolves attacked me in January... and that it was now the hour of the wolf.

I poured myself a cup of coffee and took it back to the computer, where various digitized pages were sitting on the screen.

My tin of baked goods that Abigail had given me a couple days ago sat near the computer, and I dunked a donut into my coffee before biting into it. It was delicious, as all of Abigail's baking was. But it made me think about what Liam said, about Abigail keeping her secrets the same way I kept mine. He was right, of course. I had no reason to go poking around in her life.

I just had to wonder if Liam knew more about Abigail than he was letting on.

"Focus, Harper," I told myself sharply. I couldn't let myself keep getting distracted. Liam was right. It was highly unlikely that Abigail had any sort of connection to Gail. Besides, I'd found what I needed.

Reaching into my pack, I pulled out a handful of candles and a bell. I set them up in the proper order, then summoned my magic to light them all. David had had cameras installed in the museum, but they covered the doorways and windows. I was in the archives in the basement and there were no cameras down here.

"I summon Gail Blackwood," I said into the candle flames. "I have news for her."

Gail's face flashed in the center of the circle. Then she was standing next to me. She pulled her shawl tightly around her shoulders as I stood up to be level with her.

"Well? Did you find anything?" The hope was clear in her tone, though she eyed me with distrust.

"I did," I said.

Gail's eyes widened. She trembled and nodded at me to continue.

"It's been difficult, but I think I've found answers. There were several town announcements in a nearby town that have been preserved, as well as a handful of diaries. One of them belongs to someone who was called Abigail Churchill. Who I think is Penelope."

"What do you mean?"

I pointed at the digitized pages of the diary. "She was found wandering around in the snow around the time Penelope disappeared. She had no memory of what had brought her there. My guess is that Howard Whitman's spell stole her memories and deposited her somewhere else."

"But if she was that close, someone ought to have seen her at some point," Gail protested.

"Maybe they did, but she'd changed enough that they didn't recognize her. Maybe even her appearance changed, I don't know." I shook my head. "Your searching spells didn't work because Penelope didn't know herself anymore."

"That... could be it," Gail murmured.

"I've read through bits of all her diaries," I told Gail, softening my voice as I switched to a new page. "She had a thrilling, fulfilled life. And she must have felt some connection to her past still, otherwise, why would she name her new self after you?"

Gail was quiet as she leaned over the computer, her eyes skimming the page. "It... it looks like her writing."

"I don't think she's still here. I don't think she had unfinished business, Gail. I think she moved on," I told her gently. I couldn't imagine how hard it would be to exist in four hundred years of not knowing.

Gail sighed heavily, and a waft of warm wind fluttered through the archives. "You might be right... here. The searching spell."

She held a hand out to me. I pressed my palm to hers, surprised to find that she was solid beneath my touch. She closed her eyes, and a shock jumped from her palm to mine. Instantly, the details of the spell flooded my mind. Before I could process it all, she sighed again. She smiled as she faded from view, the warmth of her departure lingering.

"Gail?" I called.

No answer. But I didn't expect one. I somehow knew she was gone for good now.

I processed the spell she'd given me and frowned. It wasn't one that I could do on my own. Maybe I could ask Ella to help me... but no. I knew exactly what I had to do.

Liam looked around at the setup I'd put together. The candles, crystals, and other ritual equipment. It was the most intensive spell I'd ever performed. It might have sapped a great deal of energy from Gail every time she performed it.

"What do you need from me?" Liam asked doubtfully.

"Stand right here," I said, pulling him over to a spot in the intricate design I'd painted on the floor. I checked the time. "We'll have to get this done quickly. Once the dawn comes, it'll be too late to perform the spell."

Liam opened his mouth, then closed it.

"How this works is that we should get a vision of what led up to Chloe's disappearance and where she is now," I explained as I took my spot. The candles were already lit and the pulse of magic was in the air. My palms were clammy as I took Liam's hands in mine.

"I don't have magic, so how is this going to work?" Liam blurted.

"I only need you to say the words and give me your energy. Are you ready?"

Liam searched my face and nodded slowly.

"Okay. Together, then." I took a deep breath and started reciting the words, Liam speaking along with me. "While the darkness lingers, let us see. With the dawning of the sun, bring the dawning of the truth. I call on Chloe to find where she is."

Wind burst through the shop. My hair was whipped into my face, and then suddenly I was back at Anabel's house. Liam and I stood holding hands in the middle of the dance floor, where Chloe was slow dancing with Trevor. I glanced over my shoulder, seeing Liam and myself in the corner as we had been only a few hours ago.

"How...?" Liam said. His head swiveled this way and that.

"Magic," I told him.

Anabel came into the room and announced the fireworks. People passed through us as they filtered out. Liam shuddered, and I squeezed his hand. "Yeah, it's not a pleasant experience, is it? But we have to follow Chloe."

Liam craned his head. "This way."

We followed her out to the front yard, but as the fireworks started, she looked around with a concerned expression. When she turned back into the house, we followed.

"Trevor?" she called.

She headed through the house, peeking first into the living room before she heard voices in a closet. I crept after her, though I knew we were making no sound. Chloe pressed her ear to the door, while Liam and I could hear the voices inside clear as day.

"—she's realizing. We can't keep this secret forever," Angelica was saying.

"Trust me, she doesn't suspect a thing."

Liam growled under his breath as Chloe flung open the door. "They are having an affair, after all."

Chloe cried out, her fists clenched. "And just what secret are you talking about, Angelica?"

Angelica's face turned white. Trevor seized her hand. "Chloe, I'm sorry. Angelica and I are in love."

"I can't believe you. I trusted you!" Chloe spun on her heel. She didn't see Trevor leap forward—

Everything went black. Liam stumbled, gasping. He clutched my hand as he groaned. "We have to stop. It's too much—"

"We have to know what happened," I said, wrapping both my arms around him. Pressure built behind my eyes, making me feel like my head was going to explode. "Please, Liam. You're strong, you can hold on."

Flashes of streetlights blurred through the darkness. It made me feel nauseated, and I groaned, biting my lips together tightly to keep myself from vomiting. Liam's arms tightened around me; now he was the one holding me up.

"It will pass soon," he promised. "It's because of the blow to her head."

One streetlight slowed, and I realized we were actually in a car. Chloe was in the backseat, hands bound with a gag in her mouth. Angelica turned to stare at her, face cast in shadows. Chloe shied back, but then the door was opened. Trevor dragged her out and marched her up the stairs. The fireworks still banged somewhere in the distance.

Trevor and Angelica took Chloe into the house, where everything went dark again briefly. When the light came back, Chloe was chained to a radiator, staring up at a basement door while tears streaked down her face.

A gust of cold knocked into me. I gasped as my eyes flew open. The candles had melted down. A wave of dizziness passed over me and I slowly sagged to the ground, Liam with me. He panted, his face ashen. Then he ground his teeth together and grabbed my hand again.

"I know that house," he said. "We have to move."

I nodded, forcing myself back to my feet. My legs shook with every step, but I seemed to grow stronger as we got outside. The first pale streaks were showing in the eastern sky. Liam pulled me to his car and soon we were off.

"So they're the ones that took her, then made a fuss about her missing so they could seem innocent," I murmured. "And so they could make it seem like she just took off."

Liam nodded, his expression tight. "Something still doesn't feel right, though. The money Chloe withdrew from her account has to be part of it. But how?"

As I studied Liam's profile, a realization hit me. This wasn't based on facts. It was a hunch... I'd been misjudging him for a long time, thinking that just because he thought little magic, it meant he was all about practicality. But he wasn't. Sure, he was skeptical, but he also understood there were more things that he didn't understand.

So what if we were misjudging Trevor and Angelica too? They were awfully quick to admit to an affair when Chloe had no proof.

"Keeping a secret can be many things," I said slowly. The pieces clicked into place and I gasped. "They were lying. Everything they told us, and Chloe, was a lie. I know what really happened!"

# 6

## DAWN OF THE TRUTH

Dawn broke by the time we reached Angelica's house. She must have seen us pull up because she was waiting at the door when Liam and I came racing up the drive.

"What are you doing here?" she snapped at us. "I'm tired. Please come back later."

Liam shook his head. "Can we come in? It's important. We believe Chloe might be in danger."

Angelica glared at the two of us. "Chloe is a flake that has flaked out on me for the last time. Please, come back later."

I held my hand open, sending my searching winds through the doorway. Angelica shivered as they brushed by her, but her attention was on Liam. I found the doorway leading to the basement quickly and slipped my winds beneath the door, tripping down the stairs. Chloe was awake, thank goodness. I used my winds to pull the gag from her mouth.

"It really is very important," Liam insisted.

Angelica opened her mouth again, but even as she did so, a faint cry rose out of the basement. "Help! Someone help me! They're going to kill me!"

Angelica jumped. Liam drew his taser and pushed his way into the house. "A cry for help, reason to answer."

A door slammed from the front yard, and Trevor raced toward us. "What do you think—"

He came to a stop as police sirens wailed. Angelica bolted down the stairs and I used my winds to trip them both, sending them sprawling, as the police cruisers pulled into the front yard. Liam grabbed my hand, and we raced for the basement door together.

"Harper," Liam said.

I knew what he wanted. I flung my hand, sending my strong winds forward. The basement door burst off its hinges and slipped down the stairs. We were quick after it, racing down. Chloe was a bloody mess, bound to radiator pipes with zip ties. She burst into tears as she saw us.

"Get the paramedics in here," Liam called to me.

He jumped down the stairs. I turned back to the front yard. Both Angelica and Trevor were being shoved into cruisers just as an ambulance pulled up.

"In here," I called. "We need medical attention."

Then I returned to the basement door, standing there to help guide the paramedics in. From where I stood, I could see Chloe bury her face in Liam's shoulder. She sobbed, clutching at him. And for the briefest, most insane moment... I felt jealous.

The paramedics came in and checked her out. She could walk under her own power to the ambulance. Liam rode with her, and I drove his car. Once at the hospital, he met me in the waiting room and took me to her room.

"You were right," he told me as we moved through the hallway. "Trevor and Angelica were stealing from her. They were worried she'd figure it out and hand them over to the police, so they kidnapped her. They figured they could drain her account and then get rid of her."

I shuddered. How awful would it be to learn that a friend was lying to you for your entire relationship? I winced and glanced guiltily at Liam from the corner of my eye.

"I'm sorry I lied to you," I whispered.

His gaze softened, and he touched my cheek. "You had every

reason to—and we'll talk about this more, Harper. I still don't know how I feel about all of this, but I know I still trust you."

Warmth blossomed through my chest. I smiled gratefully at him. He smiled back, then knocked on Chloe's door.

She was awake and sitting up when we came in. Chloe smiled stiffly at me.

"I understand you helped the detective find me," she said. "Thank you. I don't know what I'd do if... well. I'm just glad you found me."

"Angelica and Trevor won't be able to hurt you again," Liam promised. "They're going away for a long time."

Chloe nodded, letting out a shuddering breath. "Would it be too much to ask for you to stay with me for a little while? Just to be sure...?"

I grabbed two chairs and brought them over. I smiled at Chloe as I sat on one side of the bed, Liam on the other. "Why don't you tell us about what they were blackmailing you for?" I asked.

Chloe ducked her head. "It's all so stupid."

"They've already tried to cut a deal by claiming you're part of some sort of criminal activity," Liam offered. "It's best if you tell us the truth. But, I must advise you it's a good idea to have a lawyer here."

"But I'm innocent," Chloe protested.

Liam shook his head. "Innocent people need lawyers, too."

Chloe hesitated a moment, then shook her head. "I trust you. The truth is... the truth is, that business venture I had with Anabel? It didn't just go wrong. I lost everything, investing in the wrong thing. I couldn't admit it, so I hid the proof.

"Then one day I got a package, showing me all the details of what I'd done. Only, it made it look like I'd stolen the funds Anabel gave me. It was terrifying, and the message said if I gave them five thousand dollars, it would all go away. But it didn't. Every month, they demanded the same amount, which was practically my entire paycheck. I didn't know what to do."

Liam shook his head. "Which is what they were counting on."

Chloe sighed. "I guess it was. I feel like such an idiot. I should have known them better. And now..."

She closed her eyes. My gaze met Liam's. His expression softened as he gazed back at me. I sighed internally. Even if he wasn't angry anymore, we still had a lot to talk about.

....•....

"That feels like it was the longest morning of my life, let alone the year," Liam groaned as he sank onto the couch.

We were back at my apartment. My personal library of books lined every wall interspaced with the heirlooms my ancestors had left me. The couch was Abigail's old one; she recently bought herself a new set, and I bought her old furniture from her.

"So." I sat next to him. I'd wracked my brain for hours to find the perfect words, but there was only one thing I could ask. "Where do we go from here?"

Liam rested his hands on his knees. "It's only been six weeks since the spring equinox. And those six weeks have been... very difficult. I miss you, Harper. A lot."

He turned toward me. The bags under his eyes were dark, but his expression was earnest as he took a deep breath.

"I hate this. You can't know how much I've regretted that stupid notebook. I'm so sorry."

"No, don't be. You saw something weird and were concerned for me. I only wish I told you sooner."

Liam chuckled softly. "About magic."

"Yeah. About magic."

He laughed, shaking his head. "You know, even though I took part in that magic spell, I'm not sure I believe it actually happened."

"Oh." I leaned back, frowning. What did he mean by that? If he didn't believe it happened, what did he think happened? That I drugged him?

"Regardless, I care about you, Harper. Deeply." Liam searched my face, nerves breaking through his careful mask. "I won't tell anyone about this."

Warmth spread through my chest again. I nodded, unable to speak through the lump in my throat.

Liam stretched his arms over his head. "So. Now we have to talk about Abigail... did you still want to investigate her?"

I shook my head. "No. Absolutely not. You were right. She had nothing to do with what was happening, and I know that she's got a few secrets up her sleeve, but she's owed her privacy. She's a good friend, and if she has any heritage in Moonhaven... well, I'm sure she has a reason for not wanting anything to do with it."

"And as for Gail having the same name?" Liam winked at me. "You still think that was a clue?"

"Not for Chloe's case... but Penelope's, yeah," I admitted. "I told you how I found a diary from Abigail Churchill, who matches everything to be Penelope Blackwood."

"Yeah."

I smirked at him. "She married someone named Benjamin Thorne. They named their first daughter Abigail, and their son named his first daughter Abigail, all the way down to..."

"The Abigail Thorne we know?" Liam breathed, his eyes wide.

"Exactly."

Liam laughed. "I guess that wraps it all up nicely, doesn't it?"

"I guess so."

He held his arms out for a hug. I gratefully wrapped my arms around him. As we shared a tender hug, I let out a sigh of relief. Liam knew the truth and would keep my secret. We'd solved the case and saved Chloe.

Everything in Moonhaven was settled once more.

The End.

Did you enjoy *Mystic Moonhaven Mysteries*?

Please consider rating it on Goodreads, Bookbub or your favorite retailer. Reviews help me reach new readers.

Stay tuned for the next story in the **Mystic Moonhaven Mysteries.**

Have your read my other series?

*Jane and Kennedy Daniels Mysteries*

*Pine Grove Mysteries*

*Wilma Wade Holiday Mysteries*
*Mike and Maddie Mysteries*
*Mystic Moonhaven Mysteries*
*Annie Archer Paranormal Mysteries*

**Join my Newsletter for updates and giveaways!**
**www.daisylandishromance.com**

www.ingramcontent.com/pod-product-compliance
Lightning Source LLC
Chambersburg PA
CBHW020330260626
47156CB00004B/1463